One of the most prominent and best k
language, **Indra Bahadur Rai** is the a
including the novel *Aaja Ramita Chha*, translated as *There's a Carnival Today*—spanning the genres of short fiction, memoir, literary criticism and drama. He is credited with introducing fresh modernist aesthetics, as theory and in practice, to Nepali literature, and also played a major role in having the Nepali language officially recognized by the Indian Constitution. He is the recipient of the Sahitya Akademi Award, the Jagadamba Shree Puraskar and the Agam Singh Giri Smriti Puraskar.

Prawin Adhikari writes screenplays and fiction, and translates between Nepali and English. He is an assistant editor at *La.Lit*, the literary magazine. He is the author of *The Vanishing Act*, a collection of short stories.

Long Night of Storm

Stories

Indra Bahadur Rai

Translated from the Nepali by
PRAWIN ADHIKARI

SPEAKING
TIGER

SPEAKING TIGER PUBLISHING PVT. LTD
4381/4, Ansari Road, Daryaganj
New Delhi 110002

Published by Speaking Tiger in paperback 2018

Original copyright © Indra Bahadur Rai
Translation copyright © Prawin Adhikari 2018

ISBN: 978-93-86702-21-0
eISBN: 978-93-87164-63-5

10 9 8 7 6 5 4 3 2 1

Typeset in Adobe Caslon Pro by SÜRYA, New Delhi
Printed at Sanat Printers, Kundli

Contents

The Long March Out of Burma

An uninterrupted line of refugees had passed for more than ten or twelve days. The Japanese had advanced along the opposite banks of the Irrawaddy, climbed up from Tangi and reached Lasio. There was a rumour that they had arrived as close as Maina basti. Their neighbour Dhanpad Subba, a pensioned corporal, had taken his family on the road four days ago. Abruptly yesterday, Lieutenant Baghbir Mukhkiya also took off. Everybody was fleeing in hordes. The British had been retreating with their troops, fleeing from Victoria Point and Rangoon and heading for Imphal in Manipur through Mandalay. There was nobody left to resist the enemy. From early in the morning the huddle of people fleeing on foot and on bullock-carts was heading towards the dirt trail to Sumprabung. Not a dog seemed to be coming in this direction; everybody was intent on running away from here.

Jayamaya, all of fifteen years, stepped out onto the shaded verandah of her two-storey house, went back inside and sulked to her mother. She wished she could run away with all the others, and she also felt the fear that underpinned the casual levity of the situation. Subedar Shivajit Rai, sitting at an open window, had been watching the part of the road visible from his house—from dawn until night descended—for four straight days now. In the fleeing crowd were so many faces familiar and unfamiliar. He saw many old soldiers and officers from his platoon whom he had not met in years. If this day were inevitable, if it was known that someday everybody would have to flee, it should have been done earlier than this, in better days. Now he contemplated—he would not have needed to abandon any of his earnings and wealth, the house and the fields. He saw that the tea served by his wife had gone cold, clotted white.

His wife, the Subedarni, was outside, collecting the washing on the lines. He went to the landing outside the kitchen and left the teacup there, returned and called his wife. Subedarni came to him immediately.

'Subedarni,' he said in a firm voice but with a tired countenance, 'gather everything in the house. We must leave too.'

Subedarni continued looking at her husband.

'If Gorkhas have only until today to enjoy this land, so be it. But, if fortune still keeps us in favour, we will return to Machina and share laughter and joy. Jayamaya…'

Jayamaya was the first among them to tear up, and so she stood next to Subedarni, staring at a spot on the floor.

'Jayamaya, darling child, if, perchance, something happens on the road to your mother and me, go searching for your brother Bikram. He is a soldier—he won't perish. His platoon—I know—must have reached Imphal.'

Jayamaya went to her study on the upper floor.

Through the night, with the help of their servants, Subedar

and Subedarni bundled together their possessions. There was nothing they could throw away thoughtlessly. But Subedar stubbornly threw away many things. At dawn, the loading of two bullock-carts commenced. U Basu, an old man without wife or children, had agreed to drive his landlord's family up to the 116-mile mark on the Sumprabung road. Subedarni had heaped the boyish Tham U and his even younger wife with many, many gifts and given them their leave sometime during the night. Apart from the two goats and a wicker basket of chickens that were loaded onto a cart, Subedar called his servants together and told them to take away all the remaining pigs, chickens and ducks.

Early in the morning, Subedar's pair of bullock-carts joined the long line of carts trudging northward.

Because it hadn't rained for many days now, and because of the tread of the carts that had already passed, the Sumprabung road was full of dust, but, unpaved as it was, the road was wide enough for the carts to pass with ease. Jayamaya was in the first cart, sitting with the old man U Basu. Subedarni watched her home, her fields, fodder trees and fences recede, and began to sob. But the Gorkhalis who had already spent many days on the road were duelling with boastful songs, telling jokes and laughing.

The Subedar—with his large arms, broad nose and long eyes on a fair, attractive face—wearing a faded vest atop a white shirt and a pair of khaki trousers, carrying a gun, and slung over his shoulder, a Burmese bag, walked behind the pair of his carts.

It was the last week in April. Even as they walked, the sun became fierce overhead, but a scatter of clouds also showed.

The long line ahead, which seemed empty in places before, was now a thick swarm as far away as the eye could discern. By the time they reached about 6 miles away from the house Subedarni had stanched her tears. On the other cart, Jayamaya showed the old U Basu the large clearing where the entire village had gathered just a year before for a picnic; somewhere close by, she told him, was a fountain of cold water. Subedar had climbed onto a cart two carts behind his own, and was chatting with the elderly Harka Ram.

'Where are your son and daughter-in-law?' Subedar asked loudly to the old man who was about to doze off on the cart.

'Eh?' The old man leaned in with his ear and opened his eyes wider.

'Son, daughter-in-law—where?' Subedar asked again, also gesturing with his hands.

'They must have left for Manipur from Chin Hill… No news,' he said, and stared into the distance, lost in thought.

Hearing their raised voices, Garjaman Limbu said from the cart ahead of them:

'Everybody saved their skins a long time ago, long ago. Only those of us from Machin got caught in the melee. People of Rangoon and Akyabali reached Chittagong a year ago. My in-laws from Mandalay are already in Manipur. We are the only stragglers. Whoever believed those dwarves would reach all the way here? But, no worries, Subedar Saheb—we will reach there too. If we can ford the Takab-Ka, there's nothing to fear.'

Garjaman Limbu, an infamous hothead in his erstwhile platoon, whipped the bullock on the left.

'Yes, we have to go across…but I am worried it might

rain and make the river swell,' Subedar turned to look at the sky. And, indeed, there was a profusion of clouds there, as if each had been busy calving more clouds.

'Where will you head once we reach India?' Garjaman, looking ahead, merely inclined his head to ask Subedar behind him.

'Where will you go?' Subedar threw back the question.

'I'll go directly to Darjeeling. I have family there,' Garjaman said.

Subedar hesitated to give such an answer. He had travelled to Bhojpur from Burma only twice, to visit his grandmother— once eleven years ago, and again eight years ago. On the second visit his infirm old grandmother had passed away. Shivajit had considered his old country. He had realized that livelihood was the toughest of all there, and therefore had decided never to return to Nepal.

'Perhaps I will also settle there,' he finally replied.

It started pouring all of a sudden and out of nowhere. Subedar found a tarpaulin and blankets from among the bundles and gave them to Jayamaya and Subedarni to cover themselves. Rain chased sun, and sun chased rain, and a thick rain fell.

Jayamaya, hooded under a blanket, searched for a rainbow.

After another two and a half miles, the rain stopped and a clear, pale evening fell. Beginning at the head of the convoy, carts halted for the night. Bullocks were unyoked. As the dark of the night thickened, the roadside became lined with campfires.

And, once more, Subedarni wanted to cry.

Everybody took out rice to cook. The sizzle and crackle of

cooking. Some finished boiling the rice. Some even whisked smooth their dal. Somebody had brought along a tin of homebrewed beer. Subedar received a portion.

In the night, with his gun for a headrest, Subedar remembered the 224-mile long Sumprabang road, and remembered the past and the present of his own life.

Some time after the Third Burmese War, his father had arrived in Burma for the first time after joining the Burma Military Police. He had been stationed for three years at Putaw, an outpost at the terminus of this very road, where he had died. When he was in the army Shivajit had travelled to every corner of the Southern Shan province. Among those in his platoon who could swim clear across the Irrawaddy was Shivajit, and only four other men.

Morning came early in the jungle.

Bullocks were put to the yoke again. The departure was full of more bustle than the grim march the day before. Duets were being sung since the morning. Jayamaya had joined that crowd. Wilful young boys wanted to shoot down any bird that settled on the crowns or branches of trees. If they hit a mark, they would stop their carts to go into the jungle to search for it. Nobody had any fear. Everybody was laughing. It seemed the journey of a merry migration—it seemed as if they were travelling from Burma into India for a picnic.

'Is your name Jayamaya?' A beautiful, thin boy who had had to abandon his studies to be on the road, and who had been blessed with his mother's tender face, asked Jayamaya.

'Yes,' she said.

'My name is Jaya Bahadur,' he said.

Ten miles later they stopped for the night. Garjaman's cart had been left behind because his bullocks were exhausted.

'If our bullocks keep up this pace for another five days we will reach the 116-mile mark,' Subedar told Subedarni. 'We should then abandon the main road and head east towards Sumpiyang. After that, in about two weeks at the most, we will reach Ledo in Assam—there will be plenty of motor cars and trains after that. Today I'll kill a rooster, all right?' Subedar tried to bolster Subedarni's courage.

It thundered and rained all night. A thousand leaks breached the leaf shelter overhead. Drenched in the rain, Subedar took the tarp above the cart and threw it on the roof of the shelter; a fire had to be kept up all night. Nobody could find sleep that night.

The road had turned muddy the next day. The bullocks couldn't pull the cart. Rain clouds still filled the skies. Flu was rampant in the camp. Many became rain-soaked and fell ill.

All along the road carts had broken down and provisions had been jettisoned. They couldn't even advance by four miles.

Subedar had wanted to give the bullocks some rest on the next day; but an old fever returned during the night. They had no medicine, so Subedar decided to overcome the fever by abstaining from food.

In the morning there were many more carts that couldn't continue. Old man Harka Ram died in the night in his little hut. Those who wanted to leave left in a hurry; those who were resting prepared to bury the dead.

Sometime in the day Jaya Bahadur brought two pills of Aspro. Shivajit took them and slept through the day.

The sun came up again the next day. They spread their blankets over the carts and got the bullocks moving.

As they journeyed farther along the road, the number of people camping by the roadside to tend to their sick also increased. On the next day they encountered four mounds of freshly dug earth.

Those who were fleeing on foot were dying like flies.

Thereafter, all thoughts and worries fled Subedar. Everything appeared mundane.

It took them seventeen days to reach 116 miles. None of the companions with bullock-carts remained with them, and they had no recollection of when they had found the new friends who remained.

Arriving at the open spaces of 116 miles, everybody came to their senses!

There remained only a narrow trail leading towards Sumpiyang, up and away from the road. Carts couldn't navigate that trail; all possessions had to be carried. Gurkhas sat around, confused. Many had started the uphill climb. Only food and the most essential goods could be carried. Strewn over the jungle below the road were boxes, utensils, coats and jackets, bottles—abandoned and scattered. Chickens and goats outnumbered people.

Planes circled overhead, retreated.

Subedar Dhanpad Subba, who had reached a day before and was resting, cooked rice for everybody, slaughtered chickens, even presented to his guests a dry chutney with chimfing. Somehow, it felt like home.

Subedarni and Jayamaya awoke early the next morning to the sound of Subedar shooting off his gun. He had made three bundles of stuff, and was now shooting at everything else—the gramophone, the box of chinaware, the stack of records, the wall clock, the trunk, and the large copper water jar...

Somebody shot a bull. The bull carried its bloodstained shoulder and ran quite some ways before collapsing to the ground.

'Why did you kill it?' Subedar shouted at the shooter.

'Why should I leave it for the enemy?' the shooter asked.

'Do that again, and I'll shoot you.'

The man lowered his eyes when he saw Subedar's fury.

They turned U Basu back from there, and as many others attempted futilely to get their bulls to carry loads on their backs, Jayamaya, Subedar and Subedarni picked a bundle each and started uphill. The mother and daughter were also leading a goat each.

After climbing up a hill, when he looked to the heavens, Subedar saw billowing dark clouds congregated as if to ponder a grave and momentous decision. Even the slim gaps between the darkest, meanest clouds were filled with clouds just a lighter shade of darkness. Even the earth had caught fright of the impending rain; motes of dust had turned cold and heavy. Tree-tops swung and frightened crows flitted about. A small bank in the north of bright clouds was dashed with streaks of red and yellow. Above it a large sweep of dark clouds, the shape of a limbless man, lumbered forward slowly, and as if reincarnated, gained the form of a gigantic bird.

Occasionally they stumbled across clusters of a handful of houses in new clearings in the jungle, but, other than that, there was nothing to do but to trudge forward through this unending hell. A narrow path had been cut by the tread of people marching through it; otherwise, on both sides was thick jungle and dense undergrowth. After walking in this manner for thirteen days, they reached a jungle so immense where no bird chirped and no beast was seen. There, everybody felt that even birds and beasts needed the assistance of humans, that even they could survive only as long as they received human support, and that even they were scared of the bleakest wildernesses.

It was impossible to walk with cramped calves but nobody had the courage to rest for a day; everybody persisted upon dragging themselves forward. There is love for the ailing mother: after the son carried the mother for an entire day, covering just two miles, the son also fell sick. It had been raining every other day. Damp clothes had been torn to ribbons by the foliage. But the convoy continually forged forth, absent of any logic, knowledge or inspiration.

When they reached Sumpiyang they found a flat trail and everybody headed north east instead of going towards the village of Sakhen. They encountered the dead, strewn everywhere. There were even more of those who tended to the ill. Subedar asked:

'How long have you been tending to him?'

'Nearly a month now, sir,' the soldier answered.

'What will you do now?'

'I must wait, sir.'

How many more hearts could he assuage by asking such questions? Now Subedar walked on without acknowledging even those whom he knew. After six days they reached Maikhon. They had climbed over many tall mountains to reach Takab. On that day, Subedar's family walked for about a mile and a half and rested early.

Walking alone and carrying only a pouch with little

possessions, Nandu arrived in the evening. Subedar knew him. He asked Nandu to sit for a while.

'Alone?' asked Subedar.

'There was a friend,' he said. 'He fell sick, at a place five days away from here. What could I do? I carried him for a day. And then I fell ill myself. We found an abandoned godown and stayed in it. I tended to him. I don't know for how long I looked after him, waited for him. We had finished the rice. I asked people on the road for rice and kept looking after him. And everybody kept leaving—walking away, escaping. Fewer and fewer people were on the road. I thought through the night…'

'And?' Subedar asked.

'In the morning, I said to my friend—"I will fetch some rice." I came out. Didn't return.'

Subedar lowered his eyes. 'It isn't your fault,' he said. He silently considered everything for a moment. He repeated emphatically—'It isn't your fault.'

After seven more days of walking, Subedarni developed a fever. The rice was gone. For many days now they had been eating one meal of thin gruel. Subedar had lost weight, and was reduced to half. Jayamaya added her mother's bundle to her own burden. Despite the fever Subedarni walked by herself for an entire day. Everybody leaned on a bamboo cane in each hand. With the night the fever peaked. She began babbling incoherently. A rumour had reached them—a government depot had been set up in Takab to distribute medicines and rice. Subedar thought it wise to get his wife to Takab, and so he fashioned a strap with a shawl and carried Subedarni on his back.

Something akin to nature's justice, or perhaps a design conceived by the vital force out of the desperation to live, Subedarni would laugh witlessly, talk to unseen beings, unable to register pain or suffering.

Night fell. Everybody stopped to rest. But Subedar wished that night would never come. He would scold Subedarni. That night the infirm ate her fill and more, but the healthy had no appetite.

On the next day, he carried Subedarni in the same manner. He had no lingering sense of fear, but in sudden pangs a cold terror would overcome him. He would keep calling out to Subedarni, even though she was on his back, he would jolt her and call her name. Today he intensely distrusted Subedarni's sleep.

Even as he was walking, he realized that Subedarni's hands had gone cold. He put her down immediately. Subedar fell on the corpse and cried. Jayamaya howled and cried in the thick of the jungle. And, as if she understood everything but was incapable of action because of the body's insentience, a few drops of tears appeared in the eyes of the deceased.

Subedar buried the body by himself and sat by the grave. Jayamaya couldn't bring herself to ask her father to get going. Eventually, somebody else pulled them away and forced them to keep walking.

There was no count of how many more days they walked.

When they arrived at Takab, the length of the banks of the river was strewn with saris and other belongings. Takab had risen and become unfordable. Those who had arrived early had thrown themselves into the current and waded across. But a few days of rain had enraged the river. Some soldiers had fashioned a footbridge of long bamboo stalks, putting up a railing hanging from a length of rope—but it had already been swept away along with an entire family. The river that gathered in untold corners of the jungles on the mountains above suddenly unleashed here with great fury. It had a rapid current, and it was of very cold water. With each fresh wash of rain it threatened to sweep away the banks.

Rice and dal were available here, but alongside flowed Takab, as if appointed to swallow half of the population.

When his foot slipped a little under the water, a father had been lost along with the son he carried on his shoulder. When a wife panicked and made her husband panic in turn, both met their end in the river.

Around then, somebody slaughtered a buffalo that had been abandoned by the Nagas. Amidst the incessant rain through days and nights, they barely showed the meat some fire and ate it half-raw. Corpses lay scattered everywhere—nobody had the sense of throwing them down the river. They would flip a body over to scoop up the water underneath. A few dozen who had gone to fetch fresh water from the river couldn't return. Something like cholera ran slaughter through the camp.

With sunken eyes, dirty hair, facial hair grown to an untidy bush, Subedar considered the people living in squalor all over the riverbank. Ever new groups were still arriving. It was a throng of the diseased and the wounded. It rained unabated. From under all the shelters fashioned out of tarpaulins and raincoats, wet, dull wafts of smoke thinned, and as they rose, dissolved, disappeared.

A few lone soldiers still swam across the river. But the women and children couldn't cross. Five or six young men stood like stakes driven into the river and held a long, thick rope, and asking the elderly to hold on to the rope, sent a dozen people across. But when the Takab swept away those who panicked in eye-high water and let go of the rope, that audacity was also abandoned. No other option remained but to wait on the riverbanks for the rains to cease, the river-swell to ebb.

One day, Subedar walked upstream along the banks of the Takab. Jayamaya also came with her father.

The Takab became even more unmanageable upstream.

After a half mile's walk they came upon a great confluence of rivers where the river on whose banks they stood joined a river flowing in from the other side. The river on the other side was bigger, and perhaps was the Takab. But the flow of the tributary on this side overpowered the waters of the Takab—perhaps this river was deeper, or perhaps it flowed faster and with a greater force. 'If I jump into its currents, it will throw me halfway across the second river, and with a few strokes of my arms I can swim across,' Subedar speculated.

It was a much clearer day. After giving Jayamaya his coat and gun, Subedar entered the water.

And in no time, and with much less effort than he had imagined, he reached across.

Only when he shivered with cold on the opposite bank did he understand what a grave error he had made. He entered the water once more to take his daughter across. The current threw him back, wouldn't let him cross. Although he thrashed and kicked with all his might, the river swept him farther downstream. Jayamaya shouted his name from across the river and wept.

Somehow Subedar managed to return to the far bank of the river.

'Walk downstream along the riverbank. I will swim across from a little ways downstream,' Subedar shouted the instructions across the river.

Carrying her bundle and the gun, Jayamaya cried as she walked downstream. Subedar was also walking downstream, scoping for a suitable spot on the opposite bank.

At times Subedar would disappear from Jayamaya's sight. Frightened, Jayamaya would shout her father's name. Eventually, the sight of her father's white shirt would reassure her, and she would become angry with her father.

At one spot the river had pooled deep, and in another spot there were large, slippery rocks in the white water of the river, but Jayamaya crossed all of these obstacles and came downstream.

Further along was a difficult spot where she would have to skirt around the riverbank. She went around the spot and returned to the bank to search for her father. Subedar wasn't in sight. Repeatedly, Jayamaya sent her voice across the river to call for her father. Subedar didn't appear anywhere. Imagining that her father had already climbed much farther, she hurriedly ran downstream. She stood at different spots and cried and called for her father. Jayamaya was beginning to cry alone under tall, unfamiliar trees. She also realized that evening was falling around her.

Soon, the days of rains ceased and the river began to subside with each day. Soon, it came no higher than the waist.

Now all who had survived began crossing the river. After having sent so many to their deaths in the swell of the river, those who crossed easily now experienced a guilt borne of unknown crimes—as if it was a sin to continue living while others had perished.

Fighter planes would machine-gun a thin trail through the jungle. Another unending journey began onward with just that support. Jayamaya remembered nothing of this part of the journey. She remembered only one incident:

After about two days of walking she found Lieutenant Baghbir Mukhiya running in the opposite direction, unkempt like a madman. He appeared transformed and frightening—Jayamaya recognized him only from his voice.

He was screaming as he approached—'All of my people are on here. How can I go away on my own? My wife is here, my children, everybody is here. Who do I have there for me to go?'

And so he ran away, screaming...

After twenty-two days on the road, Jayamaya's group arrived at Lekhapani in Assam. When they saw in the distance a few whitewashed houses, a motor car speeding, nobody found anything to say. In nobody's heart was the joy of arriving.

Mountains and Rivers

A high mountain under constant supervision of the Himalaya. There sat a village of Nepalis: growing, becoming thick with each passing year. Home since aeons—it was also called the clan-home, the place of origin—it sat atop a hill. Old houses of stone, mud and wood. With some exaggeration, it could be called a three-storey house. Thatch on the roof: compact, neatly tied. It stood well and handsomely, that Nepali house, on top of the hill.

It was a house bequeathed by the ancestors but, in spite of all the repairs and patches, in spite of fresh plaster and wash, even from afar it was recognizably the home of poor folks who managed only a hardscrabble life. Happiness arrived unannounced sometimes perhaps during the festivals; otherwise life was the constant negotiation with a string of worries and fears: a landslip might take the house with it, or a storm might blow it down. Everybody fretted over the same questions: how solid was the ground on which the house stood? How strong were its masonry and joinery?

A dream had bound them together: that they would someday earn prosperity through a common striving, that they would share it equally, that each would have his share of plenty. But the awaking was different: always in gloom; the sun shining as if a reluctant favour. *'As if it'd lost its way here,' said Sainla, as always busy shoring up the stone wall beneath the ever-crumbling terrace.*

In this land of verdant hills and the ruby of rhododendrons, of milk-white magnolia and the gold of marigolds, in a land of colourful birds—a life of such penury seemed incongruent. Will this land forget her people and rush towards heavenly beauty? Is it aeons of poverty and ignorance that burdens the people and leaves them straggling on these mountain slopes?

'It won't do to live together anymore,' one of the brothers thought one day.

'This house will fall, today or tomorrow. None will rise from this common grave—we who have been inhabiting a common grave. I withdraw my death from the shared lot. My life will walk a separate path.

'It is impossible to arrive anywhere with this teeming multitude, this people that compulsively crawls along the trodden path. A shorter route for my branch of folks—there is prosperity awaiting us. For how much longer can we wait for a future for all? I must live in the present. I shall wrench away my present from theirs, and my future too, separate and different.'

He studied the faces of his brothers.

'I have skin fairer than his; I am different. I am darker than that one; I am different. My nose is flatter than his but higher than the other one's; I am different. I am not a pauper like they are; I am different. Neither am I a moron like they

are; I am different. I am well-schooled, I have much money.
I possess cunning.'

The gaping maw of suspicion swallows him whole: Are
we all truly of a kind? Are we indeed a common folk?

A young man and an old man.

They were climbing towards the Mahakal shrine.

The old man kept a slow but steady uphill pace. The
young man had to climb and wait, and therefore found time
to formulate and ask questions.

'Uncle, you must tell them to not go their separate way.
They listen to you.'

'Nobody listens to anybody,' the old man said. He had
paused to catch his breath. The young man didn't like the
response, but he also didn't know what he should say in return.
He merely scrutinized the sombreness on the old man's face.

'Everybody pursues their own interest,' the old man said,
still standing.

'They are the selfish ones. What could be our interest in
this?' the youth promptly contradicted.

'Perhaps their interest is minor. Perhaps we have the bigger
claim. But both are selfish claims.'

The pair walked quietly. They saw the soil and rock of the
path; they saw green grass by the wayside.

'Selfishness can also be a service. Perhaps a narrower
service, or perhaps a greater service.'

'Will the government give them reservation?' the young
man asked urgently, his thoughts having arrived on that topic.

As disappointment, this answer:

'Politicians in this government have their own interests.'

Suddenly the entrance to the Mahakal shrine came into view.

After prostrating and receiving the tika, after walking around the shrine, as he prepared to leave, the old man saw the young man reading something carved on a large bell hanging by the shrine.

'Read this,' the young man called the old man over.

'Looks like a poem,' he said with a smile.

Two short men strained to read the high writing.

Mountains
Green and flowers
Needlessly swept away by rivers.
Rivers
Bright birds
Unimpeded was their movement—
Needlessly obstructed by mountains.
Shanti! Shanti! Shanti!

The young man says, 'Hills are us, who stay behind. Rivers— those who leave.'

The old man replies, 'Rivers forever hurry to somewhere, but also always remain here. Hills are fluid and ever changing, too.'

On the day of his departure, imagining that he would never have any use for them, he discarded everything Nepali in his possession. He hurled away the khukuri, still in its sheath. Into the same corner he threw the bundle of freshly disrobed daura-suruwal and topee. Clothed in barely a stitch to hide his shame, he jettisoned over the yard the water-pot of copper and plates of bronze, the carved bowls and Bhanubhakta's *Ramayana*. 'I reject it!' he shouted in Hindi—'I reject dashain! I reject tihar too! I reject sel roti!' He trampled on pouches of sour gundruk and pungent sinki, of mountain pepper and the chimfing herb.

By the time he left home the sky had turned dark. The heavens rumbled on and on, as if to recite a string of Nepali adages.

'They were aloof even when together,' said Ranimaya, who was carrying home an armful of squash vines from the kitchen garden. She had picked long vines, to collect mature stems to feed the goats.

'I have ancient pride, I have ability,' yet another brother calculated. 'I have artistry, I have industry,' another weighed inwardly—who there was truly dispossessed? These numerous talents required protection, required preservation.

'We are the ones who really need protection!' The stack of arguments grew.

And, thus, after begging for reservation from the state, after being granted it and after receiving it in upturned palms, so many hid their departure to slink away in the night, while so many marched away in broad daylight.

Those who remain worry now—'Have we perhaps become weaker?' But that worry lasts a mere few days. Still they are in numbers large enough to revolt. And those who departed haven't really left: their bravery, talent, skills haven't left. Neither are gone the culture, the language, the nationhood, nor is absent the rhododendron flower, the fragrant magnolia and bright marigold, or the forested hills. History hasn't departed, and there yet remains a destination for the nation.

People here were attentive to whatever news arrived from the land they left behind. They took pride when they heard of revolutions and sacrifices—the land isn't without courage! Witnessing oppression, they could only feel pity.

A day in winter, after many years had passed, a day after a quake:

A beneficiary of reservations who has reached a high position in the government feels the desire to inspect the condition of those who had been left behind. *The old house must have fallen. I will see the ruins*, he thinks. *I'll shoot it with a video-camera.*

We have separated, but not parted, he thinks inwardly.

Shakes his head. As if to shake loose something inside.

Even if he flies there in disguise, like the clouds, he doesn't understand why there is always the urge to spy on the mountains.

The very next day, he has already entered a government-owned car and some controversy.

With a fellow traveller, he takes a rental car and heads for the border. With the dusk he enters Nepali territory.

'Don't talk about the history of political unification. It is only a series of conspiracies, deception and acts of oppression. If that is how the creation of a people begins, where will we get to?' he says.

'Political unification and ethnic unification, political construction and ethnic construction aren't the same things. If the political victory was a short mission over three decades, the development of our people has been a long process, spanning three thousand years. A king may harbour, on his own, the ambition for a political victory. But the progress of an entire people needs the participation of everybody,' the answer arrives.

'We are still separate creeds, separate castes—we haven't yet become a people. In truth, we are many separate tribes,' he says.

'Who do you include in this "we"? This "we" is our people. It exists. We'll survive as a people—we can—but we won't survive as separate creeds—we can't. Look at the world—have people each become unified, or have they fragmented into groups?' Another query.

'Fragmenting from unity, we are dispersed around the world.'

'But it will retain the consciousness of selfhood for aeons.'

'Reservation is not wrong. To have a nation of our own is also a sort of reservation. A people to belong to, a region to inhabit, to have a home—all are forms of reservation,' he says.

'We have the nation as a common reservation. For ages to come, we have our people, the Nepali people. Reservation, preservation, security—let's seek them on the basis of our identity,' the response arrives.

'If my gains from reservation sustain me, your troubles will be lesser,' he says.

'Your gains from reservation excludes others; our troubles increase,' the answer arrives.

After the car trudges uphill for many hours suddenly electric lights from across the dark rise fill his view.

He is startled.

'From the morning tomorrow, I'll inspect the situation.'

He has ventured out after swallowing his morning snack and sees that the people milling about in the streets are well dressed. He tells himself, 'They are inwardly hollowed by the expense of keeping up a prosperous façade.' He sees shops everywhere, 'Most of these are shops selling the bare necessities.' He sees tall houses on either side of the road. 'How many of these belong to people of our kind?'

'Cities lie about our condition, they aren't truthful,' he decides.

On the path leading away from the village he sees a healthy old woman climbing down to the bazaar with a grandson—plump and clad in new daura suruwal topee coat shoes—strapped to her back with a shawl over her forehead.

'This is some manner of travelling to the bazaar, without having to walk a step,' he looks at the grandson and speaks, seeking to address the old woman.

She pushes the knot joining the ends of the shawl over her forehead, slides her grandson down from her back, still holding him, and makes him stand. 'He refuses to walk at all, but nags about coming to the bazaar,' she says and catches her breath. 'How will I ever reach the bazaar like this?'

After more chitchat of similar nature he asks what he needs to know, 'How is life in the village?'

'Son, worries and misery, trouble and hardship come and go. But we can't stop living,' she says, as if revealing the mysteries of life itself. 'Just like a seed in the ground. A seed awakens, sends shoots upwards. But even if a rock blocks its path it doesn't despair, it doesn't give up—it refuses to die. It seeks another path. It forces its way out of the ground, somewhere or another. It surfaces to live in the sun and water and air. It stubbornly grows.'

He sees the condition of the village in the answer. This answer was the sweat-drenched smile on the village's face.

He returns from there.

He carries the grandson now, the child's legs dangling over his shoulders. The boy is iron-heavy. 'What does your grandma feed you?' he asks.

They part ways after arriving at the bazaar.

He continues his search for his old clan-home.

The old clan-home stands yet—it has even gained a new section, joined by a large stairway. A number of smaller, prettier houses surround it. 'It was built strong, this house,' he thinks, 'Why did we worry that it would have fallen by now?' Strong, bright, mirthful, capable, confident—such is the house.

No house of his own here—he is staying in a hotel room. He feels dejected, bitter here, standing before his clan-home which stands wide and tall.

'It will not fall,' he utters.

He stays for a week.

Then he returns.

'The green of the mountains is from the water in the rivers. The white in the rivers is from the rocks of the mountains… Am I raining tears?' he thinks as he watches the mountains and rivers left behind.

During his lonely return, from an unknown depth within he remembers something a Zen master once said: 'We face each other all day long, but we have never met. It has been aeons since we parted ways, but never for a moment were we separated.'

'Is life lived within the confines of knowing?' To whom can he direct his queries? He panics.

Jaar: A Real Story

'A man may cut his jaar down straight away!' Thirteen years after the death of Prime Minister Jung Bahadur, who modified this edict, a family of Samri Ghaley Gurungs migrated from Gulmi, to the west of the River Kali, to settle in Amchok, in Region Four of the Eastern Provinces. They had migrated east because their eldest son Rudraman Gurung's platoon Kali Bahadur was garrisoned in Ilamgarhi, not more than four days away by foot; and they had chosen Amchok because a Darlami Thapa Magar family of their acquaintance had already settled there.

Under the leadership of general Amar Singh, the grandfather of this Jayvir Thapa had fought the Company, and had quit the army only after Bhimsen Thapa took his own life out of humiliation. And, Shivaman Ghaley, in the Gurung year of the serpent, when he was twenty-eight years old, had fought under Jung Bahadur's command to retake Lucknow from the rebels. He was missing two fingers from his right hand, and on his cheek was a deep long gash made by a sword.

'How should I address her?' Jayvir Thapa asked in Khas, their common tongue, while visiting the newly built house of the Ghaleys a week after their arrival.

Shivaman Ghaley smiled at his wife who stood by his side, then looked at Jayvir and the Thapa wife.

'Call her your sister for now, Thapa! I become your brother-in-law then. Or, call her your sister-in-law, and you can become her elder brother-in-law.'

Ghaley and Thapa laughed together. The wives looked at each other and laughed. When the husbands laughed their moustaches shook, and when the wives laughed the dense folds of their ten-yard-long gunyu wraps shook.

'The relation between a brother-in-law and his sister-in-law is a difficult one,' Thapa continued. 'Heaven forbid if she touches him with the edge of her shawl—they'll both be forever sanctifying themselves with holy water!'

The Ghaley woman pulled her shawl over her face and bowed timidly. 'In the west, where we are from, the two separate peaks of Machhapuchre are called brother and sister-in-law,' Shivaman explained. 'Call her sister—that is the easier relation.'

'This is our younger girl—we call her Maiti,' Thapa pointed to a girl barely eleven years old. She was pretty in her black skirt and patterned blouse.

'She is our girl Devi's age,' the Ghaley wife said.

'This is my elder daughter,' Thapa introduced another girl. 'And we have aptly named her Thuli.'

Bright-faced and of a proud bearing, she was very pretty to look at. Perhaps the ancient Magar queen who died fighting the Bhotey northerners in Kangwachen looked just like Thuli.

Now Thuli stood beside her mother in a quilted shawl from Kathmandu.

'So pretty she is!' Ghaley's wife couldn't contain herself.

And now Shivaman Ghaley told his story: 'I have brought here a son and a daughter.' Thapa was aware of these facts, but he listened patiently. 'And then there is the two of us, man and wife.'

'Your elder son?' Thapa asked.

'In the army. He is a lieutenant.'

Thuli suddenly raised her eyes to look at her father.

'He will perhaps get here any day now—we've written to him,' Ghaley's wife said.

'Aren't they also building a fort in Karfok, Baba?' Thuli asked with a heart that had become overjoyed without a cause.

'Yes,' Thapa answered his daughter and continued speaking to Shivaman. 'It is easier for a lieutenant to find leave once the letter reaches him. But it is also not easy. Men of lower ranks can find a lout to take their place and run home in time to thresh new millet.'

Thapa and Ghaley laughed once more, tickled because they understood the soldier's dilemma.

By the time the Thapas rose to leave, Devi and Maiti had become fast friends. Devi had browsed through every room in Maiti's home, and as her father and sister stepped out to the yard after begging their leave, the two girls were running to see the chautara in a corner of the village. Who would stop them?

'I'll ask somebody to fetch Devi home—I'll send her home,' the Ghaley wife said to the Thapas.

The Thapa wife laughed. 'We should make them miteni friends,' she said to the Ghaley wife.

Rudraman arrived around dusk two days later.

From her home higher up on the hill, Thuli saw soldiers milling about in Thapa's yard and made a guess, and immediately knew that a sort of fear and another sort of joy had found her heart. When she sneaked upstairs to spy from the window, the Indian gooseberry tree in their own fields entirely obscured the view of the house below.

Maiti brought news in the afternoon.

'Devi's brother the lieutenant has come. Aren't you going to see him?'

'So what if he is back? As if he's worth looking at! How is he?' Thuli asked her sister as she watched the tailor who sat in their yard, stitching a dress.

'Very good-looking! He is young—not old at all!'

'Did he speak to you?'

'Speak to me? He even gave me braiding ropes! See?'

Thuli looked at the thick red string ropes in Maiti's hand.

'These are for a Limbu woman! Men never know what to buy!'

'So? What is it to you?' Maiti sulked at her sister.

When night fell, Thuli once more looked at the house below. Many men sat around a fire below the terrace of the house's yard. She could see children running about.

The next afternoon, the lieutenant came, holding hands with Maiti and Devi.

Thuli was in the kitchen behind the house, so she didn't realize anything.

It was only when her mother asked her to cook something that she came to know.

Rudraman left after staying for nearly two hours. Thuli sat dejectedly, keeping herself imprisoned in the kitchen.

When Rudraman returned after four days, Thuli found herself suddenly face to face with him.

Thuli slowly climbed the ladder. Rudraman watched her, immobile.

Rudraman chatted through the day and left only when dusk arrived. But he threw not a glance in Thuli's direction.

Maiti hadn't lied! He had the face of a hero and a keen pair of eyes. The khaki uniform suited him better than regal robes adorn a king. When Rudraman left, Thuli's heart sang—O lord! If I could be his wife, I would accept every hardship as joy, and would want no more from my time on earth!

Rudraman frequently visited over the next twenty or twenty-five days of his leave. Jayvir was mostly at home. When he wasn't, Rudraman chatted with the Thapa wife or with Thuli and left. He told tales of meeting forest-dwellers like the Chepangs and the Kusundas when he was garrisoned in the fort at Sindhuli. Then he would scare them by speculating that his garrison may shift to the malarial swamps of Jhapa and Morang. Thuli would sit and listen to Rudraman and her mother talk.

One day, Rudraman cornered Thuli and said:

'I have to get back to Ilam. Tell me if I should return soon or not!'

Thuli stood quietly, unable to say anything.

Rudraman leaned close to Thuli and brought his nostrils close to her dark hair, as if to breathe in the fragrance of her body.

'Are you shy?' he asked. 'Let's do this, then: should I stay away too long, or not? Just say, "Don't!" If you say that, it'll help me return soon. Otherwise, I may not return for a long while.'

'Don't,' Thuli said softly.

When the time came, Rudraman returned to Ilam.

Maiti and Devi had become inseparable. On some nights the girls ate at the Ghaleys' and spent the night there. Sometimes Devi didn't go home for two, three days on end, engrossed in her games, and stayed with the Thapas. The girls would clean the entire house together, make offerings to the household gods, finish chores neither girl ever chose to do on her own. When he saw the girl from the family above the hill lay claim to his home, Shivaman was touched by a strange joy and would laugh with his wife. Both families discussed their daughter's friend.

Thuli scolded Maiti a few times.

But, perhaps Rudraman would have had more success if he had tried rolling a boulder off the Tilkeni cliffs to block the Yogmai river.

And, one day, musicians of the tailor caste came to the yard and played their shehnai pipes. Platters were stitched out of fig leaves. Maiti and Devi became miteni friends. It was as if Dashain had arrived just for the pair. Devi gave Maiti a green woollen shawl along with the rupee coin bearing Queen Victoria's head that Rudraman had given her; as memento to her miteni, Maiti gave a Mahindra Malla silver coin and a stole of printed English cloth.

'You are mitenis now—don't take names when you call each other. You are one soul now, sworn to each other,' Thapa told his daughter.

'And for these daughters we have become one household,' Ghaley said to Thapa. 'Our families may not intermarry, or it'll be counted incest, and such children be chased away. We'll mourn and celebrate as one family. Our children are now siblings.'

'I accept the ways of the ancestors,' Thapa proudly proclaimed before witnesses invited by his family.

Nobody saw Thuli cry, but everyday everyone saw her reddened eyes.

Late in November of the same year, Thuli was married off to a Ruchal Rana Magar who had just been awarded the headgear for his new rank, decorated with a chain and a moon insignia of gold. Since Harshajit Rana was the son of Thuli's eldest aunt, he lay his traditional claim to marry her.

When her father-in-law and brother-in-law returned to Dhor in Region Three of the western provinces around the middle of December, Thuli had only her husband's elder sister for company. She was forced to rely upon the servants to see to all household chores. All responsibilities fell upon her.

Devi and Maiti often visited Thuli's new home with gifts from home. They stayed the day and returned.

'Don't you two ever fight! If you fight and end your friendship, I'll kill myself! I won't live…' she often told her sisters.

'She picks fights, but I always make up,' Devi would say.

'You're the one who fights,' Maiti would return the blame.

One day, Thuli asked her sisters:

'Is there news of brother returning?'

She had been yearning to ask the question, but she lived in dread of the answer.

'Which brother?' Maiti asked instead.

'Devi's elder brother. Isn't he brother to all of us now? Stupid girls!' Thuli scolded.

'Oh, you mean our lieutenant brother?' Devi said. She gave Maiti a conspiratorial look. 'Thuli, don't get mad if I say something? Maiti and I always wonder how good it would have been if you and our lieutenant brother had been married! Thuli, have we upset you?'

Thuli could say nothing in reply.

'Some time in May it will be a year since our brother went away. He will return,' the girls volunteered.

Forests shed their foliage and faraway trails showed like twisted straw. Again, one by one, all the trees in the forest regained their green. After the winds of mid-March lost their fury came a few quick showers in May.

Thuli was about to enter the house in the grey of a dusk after gathering a little cow dung on a leaf when she decided to go to the dhiki rice-press to see if the workers had finished hulling rice. The servant women had already gone, leaving behind hulled grain along with flattened husks from making beaten rice. Was someone drawing firewood from the woodshed? Thuli went to see.

Seemingly a man of the wild, Rudraman stood by the shed. As Thuli tried to run away in fright, he blocked her way with a strong arm.

'I will not kill you,' he said, grave and cruel. 'I'll ask you something. Tell me the truth: Do you like your husband? Did you marry willingly or no?'

Wide with fright, Thuli's eyes rattled.

'Answer me!'

'I married willingly. After your family and mine became avowed kin, I married willingly,' Thuli found the courage to speak, and after speaking, she felt her fear drain away.

'That kinship came later—I have a much older relationship with you,' he spoke through gritted teeth but in a voice on the verge of tears.

Thuli looked tired enough to fall to a heap and sit.

'You'll have to elope with me, or I will murder your husband. You will choose one of us. Listen—tomorrow, at this hour, I will come for you.'

Rudraman sped away from the shed. Hanging from the waist of his khaki uniform a long army khukuri swayed behind him.

Thuli fainted. But—it must have been the pain from hitting a piece of firewood as she fell—she immediately regained consciousness.

Later in the night, Harshajit applied a salve of herbs to Thuli's head.

'I wish I had died. But you would have mourned me,' Thuli said as she watched her husband. How trusting and kind was her husband! 'But, if I have my life now only to hurt you later...'

'What nonsense are you talking?' Harshajit lovingly chided her.

Thick veins writhed around his arms, as if those broad, gleaming veins pulsed thickly with love and kindness and hatred.

'No, I want to say these things to you tonight. Don't be cross. None among us holds in their hands the life they desire. Somebody, something arriving from an unseen corner ruins it.

And life is just that—which has been ruined by others, and whatever remains in the ruin. When others strike and break something whole, the splintered remains is life.'

'For me life is the absence of cowardice,' Harshajit said. He was proud of his lineage that had been elevated from Thapa to Rana after three generations of his forefathers had found valorous deaths on the battlefield.

Thuli studied her husband.

'Come home before sundown tomorrow. Will you?' Thuli asked.

'Before the sun sets these days, the moon is in the sky. I will return then. But why?'

'I want to do a small puja.'

'Keep the best bits of the puja offerings for me. And set aside lots of it.' Harshajit laughed as he walked away from the bed.

Harshajit left in morning wearing his blue uniform. Thuli had diligently polished its chains.

It was a small puja, but it took nearly the whole day. They slaughtered a freshly weaned goat kid for everybody to eat. She made the Brahmin widow who cleaned and plastered the house everyday wait through the day. When everybody left, Thuli took her favourite blouse from the trunk and gave it to the widow. She called the family tailor's wife and gave her another blouse.

She sent the servants to dig new potatoes from the field. A cow had fallen sick—she fed it herself. On her way home she found a tall pole, which she carefully arranged into the fence.

But, throughout the day, she didn't once glance in the direction of the woodshed.

The sun was about to settle behind the hills.

And now Thuli went to her sister-in-law and asked:

'Amajyu, since I have come to your home, have I made you and your brother happy? Or have I failed?'

'You are the bright light of our fortune, buhari! Why do you ask this?'

'For no particular reason,' she said, and stared at her sister-in-law.

Harshajit had returned—his footsteps were heard. Thuli went to him.

After carefully putting away his uniform, Thuli brought him water. Then she fed him meat from the puja. She saw how rapidly darkness had descended outside. After lighting lamps in every room of the house, Thuli climbed down and went outside to the woodshed.

The shed was quiet. An occasional sound from the kitchen and the dim flicker of the lamp in the niche on the outer wall of the house reached here. Her bangles clinked when she walked into a stack of firewood; a figure squatting in a corner abruptly stood.

She pulled out the long khukuri and swung it with both hands. She felt it cut into something, and the stack of firewood also fell. 'Did you come to do this to me?' Rudraman shouted.

'Aren't you yet dead!' Thuli swung hard again. She hit wood instead.

A ruckus had gone up. A bull bellowed nearby. Servants and gardener came running from the house, carrying lit lamps. From all around came shouts of 'Who is it? Who goes?' and 'Thuli! Thuli!' When she saw Rudraman in the flicker of the lamps, standing a few paces away with a gash on the left side of his back, she hurled the khukuri at him. 'Did you find no other woman?' she bellowed.

When he raised the lamp high Harshajit saw blood dripping from the gash on Rudraman's left shoulder. Thuli was trembling.

'Who is it? Lieutenant!' Harshajit asked with disbelief. 'What are you doing here, Lieutenant?'

Clutching his injured side, Rudraman looked at everyone.

'Why are you here, Lieutenant?' Harshajit asked again.

'I came to steal Thuli—to steal your wife.'

Harshajit's face swelled with rage.

'You?'

'Yes! I!'

Now Harshajit's face shrank with shame.

Thuli was crying. Her sister-in-law pulled her into the house.

'You have insulted me gravely,' Harshajit told Rudraman. 'Lieutenant—I'll have satisfaction!'

Harshajit's servants held Rudraman, surrounded him and led him away.

After everybody had gone, Harshajit paced in the darkness, and didn't step into the house. After a long while he faced the upstairs window and shouted from the yard:

'Didi, send her back to her home!'

And, without a moment's pause, he repeated his demand.

By the time a clerk had finished reading aloud Harshajit's written testimony, any trace of shame had disappeared from Thuli's face. Instead, there was disgust, anger and dejection. When the testimony reached its end, an elder who had earned the white turban of esteem looked at the Subba and other officials, then turned to address Rudraman:

'Here are assembled the four castes and the sixteen castes of both kinds of Gurungs, all seven castes of Magars, all eighteen castes of the twelve Tamang clans, and others—bearers of the sacred thread together with the drinkers of spirits. Tell us, Rudraman, are you not guilty of knowingly dishonouring Harshajit Rana? Hold your Guru in your heart and speak the truth. Here sit the Yakthumbas with Mojingna Khiwangna on their minds; Tamangs meditate here upon Maheshwor; and with Paruhang in our hearts, we are here assembled, the sons of the land...'

And, as he spoke these words, the Kiranti elder with the milk-white turban joined his palms and looked towards the Himalaya with veneration.

After a moment, after his heart and mind had descended from loftier heights to the mortal world, the elder asked again:

'Speak, Rudraman! Do you know yourself guilty? Had you indeed looked upon Thuli with false intentions?'

Rudraman stood with slumped head, as if trying to form an acquaintance with the padlocked wooden stock around his ankle. The injury on his side was bandaged but bloodstains spotted the shirt. Thuli stood at the other end, periodically glancing in his direction.

'Not only that,' Harshajit shouted, 'Thuli is a daughter of his sworn family—she is his sworn sister by relation. He has committed incest—he is a sinner! His caste must be taken away first!'

Many voices clamoured in agreement.

'Rudraman! Why do you delay in speaking? Do you

know yourself guilty, or are you innocent?' The elder asked the question for the third time.

And Rudraman looked towards Thuli.

'I am guilty.' He said no more.

Voices clamoured again in insult and anger. A spray of spit fell on his face. 'I'll bash in this sinner's head with a stone,' a Magar woman leapt. The outcry lasted long.

'You are a lieutenant with a platoon like the Kali Bahadur, but if this is how you behave, we'll inflict all manners of pain on you.' The old man spoke with an anger that welled from his depths. 'Firstly, you no longer belong to the clan into which you were born. None in our community will hereafter acknowledge Shivaman Ghaley Gurung's son Rudraman Ghaley Gurung!'

A Gurung stepped up, snatched and broke the rupa caste thread with its nine-knots; with his short knife he cut it into many pieces and trampled them into the dirt.

As this was happening, one wit from the crowd asked Thuli:

'Please enlighten the ignorant among us—which of your husbands gave you the bead necklace on your fair neck?'

Those who heard and understood the barb it burst into laughter.

'If you can stoop to such insults, these necklaces you gave me…' Enraged, Thuli broke the necklaces in one snatch and threw it at Harshajit's face.

'Return the earrings and anklets,' the women clamoured. 'Break her bangles! Wipe off the tart's vermilion mark!'

'Yes, that is right. Thuli! You have no claim to any of it,' the old man said.

Soon, Thuli lost all of her ornaments. Even the shawl on her head was snatched away.

Neither Harshajit, nor Rudraman or any other man dared look at Thuli anymore.

'Now, Harshajit, we ask you,' the Rai chief asked, 'Rudraman here has confessed to dishonouring you. What will you have done to him?'

In response came a wordless quiet from all directions. As everybody awaited the answer, a cold fear entered their hearts.

'I don't have to answer this,' Harshajit looked at Rudraman as he spoke. 'The Gorkha king's decree still stands.'

The knowing felt dread and fear.

'Do you then insist upon cutting down the man who has sullied your honour?' the Rai chief sought clarification.

It appeared as if the crowd held and released its breath as a singular creature. Many in the crowd sought to extricate themselves, repulsed by the prospect of an imminent beheading.

'If he is no coward let him offer his neck in repentance of his crime,' Harshajit addressed the four directions. 'If his courage lies only in transgressing, if his cowardice begs for life, it will be as decreed by Gorkha—let the coward crawl through under my legs. I will spit on him a mouthful of spittle and release him.'

Everybody agreed—'It is appropriate conduct.'

Thuli didn't believe that Rudraman would submit to the insult reserved for the coward.

'You have heard all, Rudraman!' the old man said. 'You have one night to think it through. Crawl under his legs to whom you have done trespass. If you say that is unacceptable to you, then it will be as will be here, tomorrow, at this very time. You have aggrieved his honour—you will be given a lead of ten paces to run. Harshajit will run you down and cut you down. If you run and earn your escape to another land—that is your good fortune. As the offender you may not strike him back. You must outrun death to live.'

Rurdaman was returned to the cell with the padlocked wooden stock still around his ankle.

It was a cold day, with a low fog hugging the ground. However hard the wind tried to sweep it away the thick swirl spun around and wallowed on the same spot.

In the cell Rudraman thought about nothing—no thoughts came. He sat and clutched his legs because his ankles hurt.

In a while, the door opened and Thuli appeared before him. When he saw the state Thuli was in, he felt remorse—I have become guilty now, he thought. But Rudraman couldn't say anything.

'Don't die. I will save you,' Thuli came to his side and spoke.

'Don't you dare do anything like that,' Rudraman growled at Thuli, mortified.

'I will confess to them,' Thuli continued speaking nonetheless, 'I will say—I have been with many more men before this. I will tell them…'

A lightning slap hit Thuli's face.

'I can't be with a woman who will confess to false sins. I can't accept her as mine.'

'Then I will go now,' Thuli turned away, her cheek red. But she turned again at the door and suddenly asked:

'Has the wound healed?'

'See it for yourself,' Rudraman said, twisting his lips with a hint of a smile.

Thuli untied the bandages and looked at the wound.

It was a deep, slanted cut, scabbed black with blood.

'Why did you cut me like this?' Rudraman whispered into Thuli's ear.

'Your sin deserved it,' Thuli said.

They fell silent.

'Mother has sent word telling me to never return home. Father has disowned me from everything. Where are you staying?'

'With my parents, but in the cattle shed,' Thuli said. 'They have given me rice. Nobody speaks to me.'

Rudraman ruminated.

'At dawn, the day after tomorrow, I will wait for you at the bridge over the Rubu. Get my khukuri from my home and walk through the night to meet me there. Can you do that?' Rudraman asked.

'I can.'

After Thuli left, thoughts teemed in his head. He was finding a new affection for life. His parents, the army, his childhood—he remembered everything. As a young boy Rudraman's uncle had removed him away from his parents, fearing that the son's birth-chart was unfavourable towards the father's, and consequently he had grown up in Ghandrung, above the valley of Pokhara. Now he recalled the sights along the Yamdi village as they had walked away from Pokhara, along the flat stretch through the fields of Subi Khet, Naudanda and the Lumle village where they had reached in the evening. Early in the next morning they would reach the Thakali market and the village of Birethanti, and after descending to cross the suspension bridge over the Madi river, after another uphill climb around noon, they would find the Sarki village. It seemed as if only a moment had passed since that day when he had watched the villagers pick barley. He and his uncle had reached the dense Gurung settlement of Ghandruk well before dusk fell. If one climbed higher still and descended after the walnut-tree chautara platform, one could see the Gyamrung river, the village of Daule, and some distance from it, the village of Chhyamrung. Under it flows the Sebung river, and, it is said, the river begins under the Ganesh Himal. In his mind he climbed higher and crossed many large passes and meadows and the jungle of Khuldi. If you continued walking the deserted paths through bamboo cane thickets you reached the cave at Hinku; and if you persisted, with a slingshot in hand and sun-baked clay pellets in a string pouch, you reached Khiledhunga. In the jungles of Khuldi he laid traps for munal pheasants with Gurung boys. Shepherds would have put away stores of firewood in the cave at Hinku; the boys burned the firewood to cook rice, boil gruel. When the snows around Khiledhunga melted, the pheasants climbed uphill. Pairs of doves flitted about. Garlic greens that had been ravaged by hailstones would repair their wounds and grow again in verdant waves.

I will perhaps never again see any of that, Rudraman thought.

'I am not the man to crawl under anybody's legs,' Rudraman declared the next day, his gaze fixed on Harshajit. An even larger crowd had gathered. 'Free my feet. Let him kill me if he can.'

Rudraman's legs were freed. He began massaging them. Harshajit held his khukuri.

They began staring each other down.

Rudraman looked around him. Nobody from his home

had come. Thuli stood in a distance, carrying his khukuri and its sheath.

'I will chase after you for seven days. And you will run night and day, with never a moment's rest,' Harshajit flashed his khukuri at Rudraman in warning.

'And you bring the fear for your life as you chase after me.'

'I will chase you alone. I will not bring assistance,' Harshajit replied immediately.

After measuring ten paces from where Harshajit stood, the officiating Subba took Rudraman to the spot and said, 'Stand here.'

The crowd had already parted to create a long, unobstructed exit.

The Subba instructed Harshajit: 'When I say—Cut him!, you run forward and cut him down.'

'Yes,' said Harshajit.

The Subba looked at the Rai chieftain, who nodded back.

'Beware now,' shouted the Subba—'By order of the laws and justice of Gorkha—Cut him!'

Harshajit rushed. His naked khukuri gleamed in the sun.

Thuli fainted in a heap.

'He escaped! He has escaped!' People had begun shouting. They stampeded away.

When Thuli came to on her own, there was nobody around her.

Thuli hurried away, carrying Rudraman's sword, a small bundle of clothes and a pouch of the flour of roasted corns.

In the indistinct light of early dawn Thuli rendezvoused with Rudraman at the bridge over the Rubu river. They ran away together.

Harshajit was not far behind—both of them knew this.

When they looked uphill after running some distance they saw that Harshajit had arrived at the bridge.

They lost count of how many rivers they crossed, how many steep mountain-faces they traversed through the day.

At times Rudraman ran a few paces ahead and at other times Thuli overtook him, and they ran right through the night.

Early in the morning, after crossing yet another river, they ate some of the flour with a pinch of salt, and drank a couple of handfuls of water, and continued forward.

Their escape lay across many mountains. Each time they reached the top of a mountain they had to run all the way down the other side, where a river waited between two mountains.

Sometime after midnight a waning moon arose. In the light of that moon Rudraman saw Harshajit walking ahead of him. Perhaps fifty or sixty paces separated them, but Harshajit was intently hurrying ahead. Thuli was farther ahead of them both.

Thuli was sitting down to rest by the wayside when Harshajit came across her. Thuli and Harshajit were both startled to recognize each other. But Harshajit did not do anything; he continued ahead.

And thus, when the fourth day had also passed and the pale evening sun was scattered through the jungle near Aulako, Rudraman and Thuli together took the lead and entered a dense underwood. Through the thicket was the mark of a narrow track, and grass taller than a man screened the sides. Further down the gentle slope of the track was a circular meadow awash in sunlight, and below it, in some distance, a small mountain river was gushing down from Chiseni Hill. In the pale evening light, in this open meadow, stood a beast, marked with orange and black stripes on a field of gold, blocking Rudraman's path.

They both saw the tiger.

Rudraman drew his khukuri and ran to the centre of the meadow.

'Buchey, any other day I would have given you the road and waited,' Rudraman, still heaving for breath, challenged the flat-snouted tiger. 'But no, I am in a rush today. You will have to give me the way. Would you attack a woman? Buchey!'

The tiger, striding towards Thuli, now turned towards Rudraman.

'Instead of dying at the hands of a man because you make me wait, I'd rather die in your jaws. It'll spare me from rotting in the jungle. Come on now, Buchey, don't keep me waiting!' He scolded the tiger like he would scold any man.

The tiger's roar shook the jungle and the evening in it. And it suddenly charged at Rudraman.

The tiger had leapt too high—it flew over Rudraman.

'That was the first pass,' Rudraman told the beast.

Immediately, the tiger jumped to pounce for a second time.

Rudraman aimed at the tiger's chest, but he missed. The tiger clawed through Rudraman's clothes and took his flesh.

'On the third pass, Buchey—either you die, or I!'

On the other side, the tiger was clawing the earth to clean the flesh off his paws.

The tiger chose a new spot on the meadow, and from there it bounded in.

Rudraman lay flat on his back and swung his khukuri with all his strength. The tiger's belly opened wide; when it fell, the tiger tried to leap to its feet, but it lay there with its guts strewn over the ground and, after a feeble growl or two, it died.

Leaning on Thuli, who had rushed forward to lend him a shoulder, Rudraman dragged himself forward.

They hadn't walked more than three paces when they turned because they heard a sound, and they saw Harshajit approaching them with a naked khukuri in one hand and a tuft of green dubo grass in the other.

Rudraman hung his head and stood there.

Thuli let Rudraman's arm fall from her shoulder and took his khukuri in her hand and stood, shielding Rudraman behind her.

Harshajit had been approaching them, but now he turned away and hurled his khukuri at a tree at the edge of the meadow. The tip of the khukuri, spinning with force, struck the trunk, chipped away a portion of the bark and slowly dropped to the foot of the tree.

Rudraman and Thuli didn't understand any of it.

'For her sake you threw yourself at a tiger—you are truly a man,' Harshajit told Rudraman. 'If your love for her is greater than the love I had for her, I am not angry at you anymore.'

Rudraman and Thuli both stared at Harshajit's face. And he continued: 'There is no rice or vermilion to consecrate the ritual with—so, with this dubo grass I make you husband and wife.'

By the end of the ceremony, in which he consecrated their bond with the dubo grass, the Rana's eyes were moist, but he wasn't yet crying.

'You are as a younger brother to me. I will take you both back now,' he said.

Rudraman and Thuli stood transfixed and lost for words.

Eventually, Rudraman spoke: 'The doors to our homes have been barred to us. The path to our land is closed. We can't live in our land without our caste and clan. Dai, I believe that just now I saw our path somewhere here. Over there—that is our path now...'

Where the river had swept away its banks, a tree had fallen across and created a bridge. A pair of men and a pair of women carrying loads on their backs crossed the log bridge and headed towards the land of the Mughals. Close at their heels an army recruiter for the Company shepherded a line of running young recruits.

Thulikanchhi

Thulikanchhi, who was between eleven and twelve years old, was slender-limbed, thin-faced, and just as fair-complexioned as Rambabu's own daughter, Parvati. She had hurried back after a brief visit home, leaving her brother behind.

'She has returned!' Rambabu welcomed her with a cry full of joy and affection and not without a hint of teasing.

'So I have.' Thulikanchhi ran into the house from the yard from where the sun had half-accomplished its retreat and where sat tiny pebbles hiding in their own little shadows.

'Did you leave early in the morning?' Parvati's mother asked a question—the answer to which she already knew. But Rambabu jumped in with mischief—because this was how he had built attachment with Thulikanchhi—and said, 'A young girl like her can get here in the blink of an eye. At her age they can snatch a bird out of the sky. She's already caught thirteen of those.'

'Very funny!' After pouting and staring at Rambabu through the corner of her eyes, she said, 'A chhurpi, aunty?' and walked up to Parvati's mother, put a yellow lump of the hard cheese on her palms, and disappeared into the house.

But Rambabu just had to call after Thulikanchhi. 'Thulikanchhi-chhori!' Rambabu appealed to her, assuming the picture of innocence, 'Nobody has given me a decent cup of tea since you went away. You always brought my morning tea. Oh, I have suffered in my Thulikanchhi's absence! Do make me a cup of thick, sweet tea!'

'Sanikanchhi must have given you tea.'

'As if that silly girl can make tea!'

'She goes to school! How can a schoolgirl be silly?' Thuli had already run into the kitchen, laughing. She could be heard pulling out a log from the stack of firewood to the floor, dragging it outside and splitting it. She also sang to herself a little.

By the time Parvati and Prakash came home from school, Thulikanchhi had finished making tea. 'Good job, Thulikanchhi! Finally, a cup of tea from your hands, just the way I like it!' Rambabu said to flatter her as he took the cup.

'Kaka says he didn't get even a cup of good tea,' Thulikanchhi said to Parvati with a laugh as she wiped her tea-scalded fingers on her skirt.

'Baba! Just you wait—if you ever ask me to make tea again!' Rambabu's daughter began sulking immediately. Rambabu had no recourse but to grin, knowing that he had painted himself into a corner, when Parvati's eyes started to well up. 'Look at her! She cries at everything!' Thulikanchhi said with a pout.

In the evening, Thulikanchhi was studying with Parvati and Prakash, their books strewn over the bed. She felt as if her bedridden father were by her side. Then she remembered her aunt. She held her breath without realizing and straightened herself in defence. She remembered her aunt's little girl and was filled with loathing. She saw her book and turned a page. She looked at every picture and turned every page. By her side, Parvati was absorbed in her sums. This made her even more reluctant to continue studying. She began chatting with Prakash.

'Are you studying or chatting?' Rambabu shouted from the next room. Thulikanchhi turned the same book to another page and started reading. Then she began reading aloud. When Rambabu came in to check on the children, she read even more loudly.

'I'll send both of you to school next year,' Rambabu said from the door. 'Both of you, in Class 4.' Thulikanchhi listened to him intently. She had heard the same thing many times before.

She asked immediately, 'If she fails her exams, how will both of us be in Class 4?'

'You'll go to Class 4. Whoever fails will stay in Class 3.' Thulikanchhi heard the answer but it didn't entirely satisfy her.

Rambabu left after lingering by the door for a bit. Instantly, Thulikanchhi stopped studying. She started peering into Parvati's exercise book instead. 'Aren't you done?' she asked, and when she didn't get an answer, she said to Prakash, 'Bed time!' She slipped under the blanket. Then she jumped out of bed immediately. 'I'm so stupid! Going to bed without giving Baba any water for the night.'

'I almost forgot the water,' Thulikanchhi said after giving Rambabu the water. 'What would you drink in the night otherwise?'

'How can my daughter forget it? My Thulikanchhi will take care of me, forever and ever.' Rambabu had already taken his shirt off and was lying in bed with a book in his hand. 'After all, my Thulikanchhi is my own little Thulikanchhi!'

'Am I, really?' Thulikanchhi managed to blurt out incoherently in her happiness before running back to her room.

'Who was that, a few days ago, in the bazaar, what was it he said?' Rambabu asked Thulikanchhi from his room.

'I've already told you!'

'What did he say, again?' Thulikanchhi was pushed to answer.

Thulikanchhi didn't climb into bed, and she didn't turn towards the door either. She stood aloof, swaying a little.

'A man,' Thulikanchhi told the story. 'He saw us wearing similar skirts and said, "You must be sisters."' She had had to try really hard to contain her laughter the previous time she told the story.

'Of course you are my daughter! Your face is just like mine. You have just the one nose, just like I have one nose, and just the two ears...'

She found Rambabu's joke unpleasant.

'But your nose isn't like Baba's,' Thulikanchhi said to Parvati, and they were soon comparing themselves. When one lost a contest, they both laughed. Thulikanchhi regarded herself: large, jaundiced eyes, lips larger than the mouth, and a scrawny neck. The fact that both the brother and the sister had names beginning with a P was also discussed, and it was suggested that perhaps she could also take on a similar name. Upon Thulikanchhi's insistence, they went back to competing on the lengths of their hair.

That night, long after Parvati fell asleep, as Thulikanchhi floated between sleeping and awaking, she imagined a day far in the future when Parvati would be married off but she would stay behind, living in the same house and taking better care of it.

Rambabu had just reached home after making a round of his fields in the morning when he heard the neighbour woman rail about how Parvati and Thulikanchhi hadn't let her son fetch water from the communal tap. It was a small matter, but Rambabu grabbed Parvati and began hitting her. He was a weak man, so when he had struck her a few times, he could not rein in his rage and he began hitting her with greater fury. The house filled with shouts and cries. When Aama tried to pull Parvati away, she too received a scolding. Thulikanchhi swept all around the house in a flash and began methodically fetching water from the tap above the house.

She left the bucket under the tap and stole closer to the house to listen attentively to the sound of Parvati crying in the house, and to Rambabu scolding her periodically. Although she was glad to have escaped a beating, dissatisfaction pooled somewhere in her heart. She went and stood by the tap once more. Water gushed ceaselessly from the tap and foamed on the rising surface of the water in the bucket. She kept staring at it, enrapt, for a long while. Water gushed out from the over-brimming bucket but she didn't hear it. She stared at the spilling water, uncomprehending…

While returning from the field after fetching and pouring out the bucket of water, she leaned towards the house and listened. The house had gone eerily still, as if everybody inside had killed themselves only moments before.

She climbed above the house and found a slender stem. She set the bucket by the path, looked around, picked up the stem and hit herself on the calf with it. She hit herself as hard as she could a few more times, stared at the thin stem, then hurled it down. When she walked on with the empty bucket, she was filled with the determination to carry Parvati's share of water also.

In the evening, remembering that Rambabu would arrive early from work, Thuli brought him tea. 'See? My Thulikanchhi remembers that today is a Saturday,' Rambabu said, like the grown-up that he was, already forgetting the morning's incidents.

'You flatter only when you get your tea,' Thulikanchhi spoke of what had been occupying her heart. 'But when you see me in the bazaar you don't even speak to me.'

'When did I not speak to you?'

'Today.'

'Today! Where?'

'Where else? In the bazaar.' Thulikanchhi said with a bit of acid in her voice. 'You were standing to this side of the warehouse in the bazaar. You were talking to three big men and laughing. I called out to you, but you didn't talk to me.'

They had been discussing Jalpahar and laughing.

'So, you called me by my name, did you? Why didn't you pull my sleeve?'

'How could I?' Thulikanchhi scolded. 'I called you, I said, "Uncle!" twice, from the other corner. But you were deaf, and you kept talking to someone in a coat just like yours, and laughed and laughed…'

'Forgive me! Please forgive!' Rambabu spread his hands.

'Smaller portion of meat for you tonight!' Thulikanchhi said and skipped to the kitchen. She began cutting up the meat. After a while, she heard a murmur in the adjacent room and went to eavesdrop.

Rambabu was sitting on a low stool and showing affection to Parvati, pleading with her. Parvati had her arm over her eyes and with intermittent sobs was giving continuance to the sequence of tears and weeping that had been disrupted in the morning. Rambabu was lovingly caressing her on the places where he thought he had hit her in the morning. Thulikanchhi shrank into the darkness by the door and watched them.

'Don't cry, my daughter! Don't cry!' Thulikanchhi heard. 'I am your father! Of course I'll hit you sometimes,' he was saying with love. Parvati's sobs didn't stop. Once more, the father tousled the daughter's hair and his hands wiped away hot tears from her cheeks. Thulikanchhi walked away on tiptoes.

In a bit, Parvati came to the kitchen. Thulikanchhi saw how her face beamed with immense arrogance and pride. Thulikanchhi kept at her chores and didn't say a word to Parvati.

In the morning, Thulikanchhi woke up, lit the stove and boiled water for tea. As she was washing her face, Parvati also came out to wash her face. She had returned to the kitchen and was making tea for Rambabu when Parvati said, 'I'll give him the tea.'

'How does it matter who gives it to him? I'll do it myself,' Thulikanchhi said.

'But today I'll do it,' Parvati shouted.

'You don't need to try to be his pet. I woke up early in the cold, I lit the fire and made the tea. Now she wants to act smart!'

'Why are you fighting?' Rambabu, who had woken up, shouted.

Parvati snatched the bowl and walked away. 'I haven't added any sugar yet!' Thulikanchhi sprang up to grab the bowl and carried it away, stirring in a spoonful of sugar.

Rambabu was sitting up, seething.

'Do you have to fight so early in the morning? You're the older—can't you be more understanding? What harm was there in letting her bring it?'

She stood there, frightened.

But much later, when the emotions ebbed, a corner of her heart filled with sadness. The sun had barely warmed the air when she went behind the house and slumped over, all alone.

She ignored Prakash when he came to say, 'Thulikanchhi! You've been told to sweep the yard.'

In the afternoon, after she had cleaned the plates and other dishes with Parvati and put them away, Thulikanchhi climbed down to the alder grove beyond the terraced fields. The pain and the joy of revenge flooded her heart once she decided that nobody had seen her steal away, and that nobody was watching her. There was rage in her heart.

Worried that someone could see her from the house, she climbed further down and found a lovely hollow in which to hide. She shrank into herself and took small breaths.

'Let them think I have gone away.' Her heart ballooned with happiness. She felt loved. Now she recalled how she had carefully hidden her tin box of possessions under the stack of firewood, and now she laughed as she imagined the look of astonishment on their faces. 'They'll think I have run away with my clothes and my box.' Once more, she felt wanted, and felt joy.

But even after a long time, nobody came searching for

her. The hollow was getting cold, so she moved out and sat in the sun. She heard something—perhaps somebody calling from the house. She tried to listen carefully, but couldn't hear anything. Dry twigs were strewn everywhere around her. She gathered a few and kept them by her side.

'Thulikanchhi!' Parvati really was calling for her now. 'Thulikanchhi!'

She scurried back to her hiding place. She giddily giggled to herself and found a place even more hidden for her to crawl into.

A long time passed but nobody came from the house, nobody called out to her. An empty silence continued to ring in her ears. Defeated, she emerged again and found the sun which had moved far from the hollow. The ground where she sat was overrun with weeds. She pulled them out. The sun skirted around her and set for the evening.

'He shows love to his daughter!' She became angry inside. The scene from the previous evening came to her mind and stayed there for a long time, despite her attempts to get rid of it. She had been living with the family for a while now, but she had witnessed the scene of affection only on the previous day. Maybe Rambabu will come searching for her, and show love for her, too. She gathered some tears in her eyes and bowed her little head. 'I'll also cry,' she told herself, imagining herself in Rambabu's arms. She lost herself to the warmth of that joy.

A dog emerged from somewhere to run past her and break her reverie. The silence seemed additionally desolate, and the air colder. Flashes of the dream of Rambabu climbing down to find her and lovingly leading her home kept coming and retreating. The hope and desire that Rambabu would pick up the bundle of twigs that she had collected and lead her away with a hand on her shoulder increased momentarily and, in that delusion, she looked up the steep path. Above her were silent bushes and brambles and nothing more.

Somewhere in the distance, two women chatted and laughed as they walked past, and soon they too were lost. Thulikanchhi got up, started picking dry branches and twigs scattered around her and, without a glance at the steep path that led to the house, gathered as much firewood as she could. When she had collected a large stack, she took her scarf and tied the wood into a bundle, set it on the edge of a terrace, secured the load to her forehead, and headed up the hill towards the house.

'They will say I had gone to gather firewood,' she assured herself.

My Sister

'Although I am a Christian, I like the festival of Tihar, and especially the day of Bhai Tika. Therefore, I have accepted someone as my sister, and go to her each year to receive the tika from her. Didi, my sister, fasts and waits for me. When she sees me, her face lights up with joy. When she seats me down on a woollen rug and makes the three circumambulations, when she protects me by breaking Yamaraj's head in the form of a walnut, when she puts a beautiful tika in red and white on my forehead, when I get to wear a garland of bright marigolds, I lose myself in a surfeit of bliss. I forget that I am the son of Christians; the joy of knowing that I have a sister and that I am her brother floods my heart; I put my forehead upon her feet in supplication...'

The jeep had passed Jorbangla, and was making its way along the straight road towards Simkuna in the pale light of the morning. Along with the driver and Krishna, the speaker was the third person in the jeep. Krishna had just met the man with a good-looking and clean face, hefty of build, wearing a hat, and with dim eyes, but, perhaps encouraged by Krishna's garrulous nature, the man continued to narrate his story:

'I had reached Class 8 that year. But I was very bright in mathematics, and through the winter I used to go to Haridas Hatta to give math tuitions to Rejina, a girl who was also studying in Class 8. We used to tackle cubes and solutions and such in algebra.

'Another girl—somewhat older—would sit and watch the two of us. I heard later that her name was Kamala, and that she was in Class 9. When we became better acquainted, I started calling her Didi. She too started calling me her brother. I would visit Kamala-didi's home. Her father had some sort of a job at the court; he was frequently transferred—sometime to Kharsang, sometime to Darjeeling. I also talked to my friends about Kamala-didi. They praised her simplicity. At home, I told my grandma, my younger brother and mother that I had accepted someone as my elder sister. Perhaps I talked about her too often, because mother laughed one day and said, "You keep talking about your sister. Bring her home some day—let's see what your sister is like!"

'After a few days, and after a lot of persuading, I brought Didi home. Grandma and mother liked her immensely. Grandma said, "Your uncle had a daughter just like her. Same age, too. She died suddenly after complaining about a headache. She had just as bright a face."

'I received my first tika from Didi's hand that year. I presented Didi a rupee note and a copper coin. I realized after giving her the money that my hands had become covered in sweat. I touched my forehead to her feet, ate rice and banana and sweetmeats. I stayed there all day long, browsed through Didi's books. Kamala-didi didn't have a mother—she had died long ago. There were two younger brothers at home, but both were my juniors in school. I returned home only at five in the evening. As I left, I picked the largest of the garlands hanging there and brought it home.

'That year, Didi passed her exams and reached Class 10, and I reached 9.

'Christmas arrived. My Christmas would be incomplete without inviting Kamala-didi. My brother and I went to fetch her. We ate cake, oranges and meat. "This is the first year, and so we—your brothers—came to invite you," I said to Kamala-didi. "But, from the next year on, if you really think of me as your true brother, you have to our home uninvited." Aama also supported what I was saying. "You are now brother and sister, and may you always remain brother and sister," she said.

'Clad in a white cotton sari and draped in a large white woollen shawl, Kamala-didi laughed by the hearth in a daze.

'Around May of the following year, Kamala-didi's family moved to Kharsang when her father was transferred there. She enrolled in a school there. She would write to me with advice and counsel. Her English was excellent. I would also reply with a diligently chosen vocabulary. It was in Kamala-didi's letters that I first read phrases like "A thing of beauty is a joy forever" and "Our language is our civilization".

'And such was my fate—I couldn't go to Kharsang for Tihar the following year to accept Bhai Tika blessings. I wrote to Didi, asking for her forgiveness.

'When Didi was "sent up" for the finals by the school, I received a letter with the news. I was busy with one task or another, and I failed to respond in time. When, nearly a month and a half later, I found her forgotten letter in a notebook, I wrote a hasty reply. No response came.

'Many months passed. I occupied myself with my studies and in volunteering around the village. My brother occasionally teased me and said, "You forgot her, and your sister has also forgotten you!" I would smile in embarrassment. I had nothing to say in my defence.

'Then, I ran into Kamala-didi's brother at the cinema one day. "When did you arrive, Bhai? How is Didi, and everyone else?" I asked.

'"Didi fell very ill," he said. "She couldn't sit for the finals. Now she manages to walk a little to sit in the sun outside."

'"So—she didn't sit for the finals?" I must have asked again in my agitation.

'"Buwa has said she should study at the same school this year."

'I stood amidst the milling crowd, transfixed.

'"Come by the house before you leave. Take Didi a letter from me."

'"I will come by at eight o'clock tomorrow morning, Daju." He said a namaste, and went in. I kept thinking about Kamala-didi throughout the movie. When I reached home, I immediately told everybody about Kamala-didi's illness.

'I wrote a letter.

'In the letter I wrote: "I met your brother today and heard from him how you had fallen ill, and how you have become better now. Everybody here feels sorry. Moreover, it makes me even sadder to hear about how you couldn't sit for your finals. But, Didi, a delay of a year is insignificant. Please put your heart into your studies. I will also apply myself to my studies. I am no longer just your younger brother. I have grown into a young man. We will both pass our finals next year and go to college together. Didi—the future is bright; look to it!"

'My letter received no response.

'It had already started raining incessantly in Darjeeling. Through such rains the boys carried the ornate Muharram taziya tombs to Kagjhoda. The holiday of 15th of August arrived. Buildings around Chowk Bazaar appeared a dark mass of people. The next day was a Sunday, crowded with shoppers. And there was a speech at the marketplace on the same day.

'I was getting my hair cut at the barber's. On the tall mirrors before and behind me I could see people come and go on the street outside. As the barber cut my hair, I lost myself in watching the mobile spectacle.

'Some five minutes later a young woman appeared on the mirrors into which I had been gazing. She was very dolled-up. It occurred to me that she might be Kamala-didi, but I couldn't believe it because of the amount of make-up on her. She was wearing a sari and carrying a purse, and also a parasol. I stopped the barber for a moment. The young woman climbed downhill and walked right past the barber's saloon.

'The barber started cutting my hair again. I wondered in amazement about who the woman might have be. Suddenly, the saloon drapes rasped open.

'"Bhai…!" she cried out.

'I was astounded. The person indeed was Kamala-didi, but with her hair piled sky-high, red rouge thick on the face, garishly bright lipstick on the mouth, flashy earrings on earlobes—I couldn't find the words!

'"I had gone to your house. Nobody was home. Your little brother said you had come to get your hair cut. You haven't forgotten me, have you, Bhai?" she said in a shrill voice.

"'It was you, Didi, who didn't reply to so many of my letters," I finally managed a few words. "When did you return, Didi?"

"'It's been a while, you see—nearly a month now!" she spoke in a strange manner. Her eyes had become wide and flitty. Then she twisted her face oddly and said, "I came to invite you, Bhai."

"'Invitation to what, Didi?" I asked.

"'There is a recitation at our home tonight. You have to come, no matter what. Bhai—you have to come! Here's the betel nut for the invite…"

'I was taking my hand out from under the white apron when she scolded me, "You don't have to take your hand out! Keep your hand inside the apron. You'll get hair all over your hand. What did you learn from your hygiene class? Open your mouth. I'll put it in your mouth."

'The manner of her speech and her voice were entirely changed. I quietly opened my mouth. She stuffed it full of betel-nut wedges.

"'Come in the evening," she repeated.

"'Yes, I will. When should I come?" I asked.

"'The puja is at seven, but you should come earlier. Can you come by four?" she said.

'She finally left after another fifteen minutes.

'As I was paying the Muslim barber after the haircut, he asked me, "That girl from earlier—is she all right in her head?"

'I said, "That's just how she is. She is my own sister."

'I bathed and reached Didi's home exactly at four. She still hadn't returned from the bazaar. I sat chatting with Babu—that is how I also addressed Didi's father. The Brahmin priest arrived shortly. I expressed regret to Babu that Didi had fallen ill and missed out on sitting for her final exams. "In her case, son," he said, "it was as if she fell ill because she wanted to avoid sitting for her final exams. When her friends finished their exams and came to visit her, the illness that hadn't been cured by so many treatments and medicines began to cure itself. And she also became unstable. I had just remarried. All over Kharsang she earned me the blame that my new marriage had driven her to insanity. She would shout all manner of things at people who came to visit. I didn't tell anybody about her because I had hoped she would die soon."

'Kamala-didi arrived just then.

'The chit-chat died.

"'Ha! My brother is here!" She laughed and shouted from the door even before entering the house. "Babu—my brother will stay here tonight, he won't go home. He'll sleep with me."

'My earlobes turned red and hot. My face flushed warm.

"'Go, Chori—make tea for your brother. You have some, too, and give some to the priest. It will get dark soon. We have to hurry," Babu lovingly instructed her.

"'Come, Bhai, come with me," she said and pulled me to the kitchen. There was much I wanted to discuss with her, but she asked me all sorts of questions and didn't let me get a word in edgewise.

'The recitation started at nightfall. Many neighbours from up and down the hill had been invited. A tarp had been put up over the yard; banana plants in its four corners held a canopy with a full vessel of water under it. We sat on woollen blankets and listened to the stories being recited, shouted "Jai!" in unison and threw the offering of flowers onto the canopy. The penniless woodcutter had already completed Shree

Satyanarayan's penance and become prosperous and fulfilled. Kalawati, the daughter of a trader, had undertaken Shree Satyanarayan's penance to protect her father and her husband while they travelled abroad, and now, hearing that they were making their homeward journey without ever having faced any calamity, she ran madly in their direction, neglecting even to partake in the prasad wherein was contained the grace earned from her worship...

'Kamala-didi stepped over the people assembled there to come to my side.

'"Bhai—come with me. I need to discuss something with you," she said.

'I stood and followed her obediently.

'Everybody was staring at us.

'When we reached her room, she latched the door from the inside. She came close, stood before me, and, suddenly, with heavy breath, asked, "What is in your heart? Tell me the truth—what is in your heart?"

'I wasn't prepared for such a question. I couldn't even follow her question to begin with.

'"What would I have in my heart, Didi? I have nothing in my heart," I said.

'She was scrutinizing me with dark, alert eyes. I thought her eyes would discern even the faintest motion of the hem of my shirt.

'"In your letter you..." she started again. "Do you know what you wrote in your letter? I am no longer a boy, but I have grown into a young man... What does that mean? It has a meaning! If you comprehend it, it has a profound meaning..."

'"I didn't mean it in any such way, Didi! You are as my own

sister. I have taken the Tihar tika from you. I have touched my forehead to your feet."

"'You're a Christian and I am a Hindu—how can we be brother and sister?" Kamala-didi blurted. "Don't carry on this pretence. I see right through your heart."

'I unlatched the door and came out. And, without turning back even once, I reached home in fifteen minutes.

'From that day on, I stopped going to her house.

'I was climbing down the steps beside Maalgodam when I suddenly spotted her. She was even more garishly made-up. I turned and ran uphill.

"'Bhai…!" she was calling out from below.

'I would no longer mention her at home anymore. If mother or anybody else brought her up in a conversation I either went off to my room or went away from home entirely. It astounded me to wonder how she had come to be the way she was now. But, if I thought of her appearance it frightened me, the body shuddered and the mind was overcome with revulsion. If I ran into her younger brothers on the streets I merely smiled at them, but didn't chat with them. When I met her father I made small talk and escaped. "Son, you don't come around anymore. What keeps you busy?" he would ask.

'The school closed for the Dashain holidays. I would pray for Tihar to not arrive, and if it did arrive, I prayed that I would be able to escape it by being forced to go somewhere else. I would add, "Lord, grant me strength!" Dashain passed and the school reopened. I would try to busy myself with studies and forget the other matter. When I awoke after a night's sleep I would find myself wishing that Tihar had already come and gone, and that it was already time to go to school. After a few days the Tihar holidays began.

'Countless lights were lit in the bazaar area for Laxmi Puja. When we returned after watching the illumination, a half dozen young girls were still singing outside our neighbour's door where a few candles still flickered, blessing the Chinese man and his Nepali wife inside.

'At home, Aama asked—"Have you sent word to your sister that you'll go to receive her blessings? Make sure you remember to go this year. Go early in the morning."

'I didn't answer.

'At around eleven o'clock on the day of Bhai Tika I headed towards Didi's home. I had taken my younger brother along but my heart was also filled with dread.

'Kamala-didi hunched over in the sunlit yard of her house, her hair in wild disarray, staring into a large bowl of water. She didn't realize that we had arrived, or perhaps she didn't care: she was lost in such deep thoughts. We greeted her stepmother and Kamala-didi yet continued to brood. We stood there, taking care to stay out of her sun.

'Her stepmother shouted into her ear, "Your brothers have arrived. Give them the tika. They are standing here. Get up!"

'"Oh, my brothers are here?" Didi said, startled, but didn't look at us at all. "I will make tea."

'She didn't even glance in our direction before going inside.

'I had become apprehensive. I approached Didi's stepmother.

'"How is Didi?" I asked quietly.

'She made a wretched face.

'"Like she always was. Sometimes she seems fine, but sometimes she goes raging mad and makes it impossible for us."

'"Are you getting her treated?"

'"Nothing has worked. We even got the shaman. The doctors only took our money."

'We sat outside and chatted about other matters. She also asked, "Son, do you know a boy named Jivan?"

'"Many people are named Jivan. Why?" I asked.

'"It seems this Jivan used to write to our Kamala."

'"Where is he from?" I asked again.

'"Must be from the tea gardens," she speculated.

'A faint memory came to my mind of Kamala-didi walking with a boy.

'"Maybe…" I said tentatively.

'It had been a while since Didi had gone inside to make tea. I told my brother, "Go around the back and look into the kitchen."

'Didi's stepmother was silent, lost in thought.

'My brother returned in a hurry and angrily said to me, "Why did you send me? Why don't you go and see for yourself?"

'"What happened?" I asked, but my brother wouldn't answer.

'So I got up and, making a show of clearing my throat, went towards the kitchen.

'When I reached the door I saw that the stove was still cold, absent even of kindling prepared for the fire. She had climbed atop the clay stove, draped only in a sari, and was busy drawing maps of India with a piece of coal all over the kitchen walls, marking regions that grew barley and wheat, regions with mineral abundance. Eight or ten maps had already been completed. She was intently drawing the maps, unaware of my presence at the door, watching her. My eyes stung with fresh tears.

'I walked back quietly. I said to Didi's stepmother, "We will leave now, Aama. Didi's condition has deteriorated. Let this year be, but I will come back every year."

'Such was that year's Bhai Tika.

'I was sent-up from the school for the finals. I sat for the final exams and passed. My heart would sour whenever I remembered Kamala-didi's condition. But, that seems to be the extent to which most people can show sympathy.

'One day, I came home from college to find her sleeping in my bed.

'I was scared inwardly, but I also became angry. When I asked my mother, she said, "Your sister is lying down for a bit because she has a headache. Let her sleep for a while. Don't wake her."

'"Aama—you don't understand!" I shouted.

'"Let her be! She said she wanted to sleep in your bed. What is so wrong with that? It isn't as if you're going to study right now!"

'The things my mother would say!

'I was blind with rage. I left and walked towards the library.

'When I returned at night she had already left. My brother and I discussed the recent Bhai Tika at home for the first time. Grandmother, mother and everybody else pitied her, clucked with sympathy.

'She returned early the next morning!

'"Bhai…!" She called out to me in a strange voice. "I need you to help me with something. Will you?"

'I asked in a voice quivering with fear, "What sort of help?"

'"I have written a long letter to your brother-in-law, a long one. Read everything in it. After reading it, send it by post. I will give you whatever money you'll need. But you must do this!"

'Before I could say anything she took from her red bag a sheaf of papers, some thirty or forty pages thick.

'"Read all of it first. Finish reading it by the evening. I will return tomorrow, and the two of us can go together and drop it off at the post-office."

'"Okay," I said, wishing that she would leave immediately. 'And she did leave immediately too.

'Her appearance was even more disarrayed than usual. But the smell of unwashed hair and fragrant hair oil somehow stung my eyes.

'I read the letter. All the pages were written in safflower-coloured ink, like that of a copying pencil. At the beginning was written (her spelling, and her own underlines):

Memories of my past!
Prince of my heart!
I dreamt of many, many smiling blossoms blooming in a garden. Innumerable bumble-bees visited to bring them ecstasy. Dark bees caressing the flowers delicate as eyes appeared not at all pleasant. <u>But a blossom in a corner cried mournfully. I was that forsaken blossom.</u> From the blue sky came buzzing a bee. <u>That was you, my darling!</u> When the blossom saw the bee she smiled shyly...

'I couldn't read any further; I was embarrassed.

'The next day, I told her that the letter was "very sweet". We asked for a special envelope to be made at the shop. The envelope alone cost thirty-six paisa. When the letter was weighed at the post-office it required one rupee and sixty-five paisa just for the postage stamp.

('When I met Jivan later and asked him, he said that his elder brother found the letter first and opened it, assuming it was a magazine. "Bhai, that poor lunatic sent it to me for no reason. I am a married man, with wife and children. There never was any romance with her," Jivan said.)

'And I also pitied Kamala-didi. If only we could get her to a good doctor, she would be cured, I would think. I read in a book that such patients benefit a lot from being taken for solitary walks and having sweet little stories read out to them. Out of concern for her I read quite a few books on psychology around that time. I even took her a few times for walks through desolate, quiet places. But her appearance and speech had become otherworldly. Although I was also determined to put all my effort into saving her right to the end, every now and then she would end up doing something or other that was utterly indecorous. I couldn't look her in the eye. I was saved by my dharma alone, from once having put my forehead to her feet.

'But, man is a selfish being.'

Having said this to knot up his heart the man went silent. The jeep had climbed down much farther past the rest-stop from where the confluence of the Teesta and the Rangit is visible. After crossing many more turns on the road in silence he started again:

'Man is a selfish being. I became selfish, too.

'After a long romance with Rejina we exchanged engagement rings.

'I started becoming scared now—lest my love and marriage be ruined because of this evil, deranged woman. I became greedy for my dream of bliss. Who knows—some day, suddenly, a small incident could occur which would destroy my dreams of a blissful future. I became determined to never again appear before her.

'They said she'd come around. I was never at home.

'She continued to visit. She came around for nearly a month.

'I instructed mother to make up an excuse to make Kamala-didi stop her visits. Her visits to my home were scandal to me.

'Finally, one fateful day, mother and others beat her and chased her away. She bled after cracking her head.

'And, at her own home, she received the total bondage and suffering reserved for a mad woman.

'And time flew past at its own pace.

'After four years, I was passing through Kalimpong on my way home to Darjeeling from my in-laws' place in Gangtok. When the driver we had arranged for made us wait for too long I went searching for the hotel where he regularly ate to call him to the jeep. The driver was eating. I had just told him to hurry up and was about to return when a familiar old voice called from behind.

'"Bhai…!"

'I didn't have the courage to turn around and look. My bones turned to jelly.

'"Bhai…! Do you recognize me?" She asked, tugging at my sleeve from behind. "Bhai—Did you recognize me?"

'I turned around and looked. It was her. But, on that day, she appeared normal.

'"Bhai," she started again. "I seem to have made you suffer, embarrassed you with what I said. Bhai—how can I explain it to you! They say I was ill, Bhai! Of what I did then, I have no recollection, as if I had sleepwalked through everything, I remember nothing. The little I do remember doing, I don't remember why I did any of it. I am telling the truth, Bhai—please believe me! The doctors cured me. Father got me married off. I don't remember anything. Bhai—your sister is begging your forgiveness."

'I looked into Kamala-didi's face. And, really, the expressions on her face were different. Her voice rang of truth. It wasn't the face of embarrassment at remembering all the transgressions committed knowingly; it was a face that was drained bloodless out of fear of my incredulity. I, too, wanted to apologize for my deceitfulness and cruelty, but I found myself speechless.

'"Bhai—this hotel is mine. Your eldest niece—she is over there. Your brother-in-law has gone to the bank on his own business. Sit Bhai, drink a cup of tea from my hand before you leave."

'Tired with the joys and turmoils of the heart I sat down on a bench.'

He had finished his story by the time the jeep climbed down to the Teesta. Krishna was lost in thought in his seat. He was supposed to get off by the Teesta and walk to the town. Even after getting out of the jeep, Krishna continued to stare at the man. He wasn't looking at Krishna.

'Drive on! Let's get going!' Krishna heard him instruct the driver. 'Today is Bhai Tika for everybody. My sister is waiting for me.'

Chaprasi

Ramlal the chaprasi was immensely proud of his son's fine education. His son Ajay, however, often felt the shame of having for his father someone who wore a coat of thick, black cloth, drawstringed suruwal, and a red cotton turban as his uniform.

For years, Ajay had been convincing himself that there was honour in a chaprasi's job. There are hundreds of jobs just as honourable as being a chaprasi, and thousands more jobs are beneath it—are they all bundles of shame? Ajay had often repeated this line of logic in his heart. He was a clever boy, and this year he had passed his high-school finals without ever once failing his classes. Ajay was also well-built and good-looking. But, if in the course of a conversation anybody inquired about his father's line of work, he would lose his voice and would reply quietly—'He works as a chaprasi.' And when people went quiet for a moment after hearing this, he would see the grave insult and pity in their reaction. His conscience would put constables, bearers, watchmen and gardeners in the same category as a chaprasi, but his heart would find his father's black-and-red uniform the most unfortunate of all.

'Let Babu wear his uniform only when he goes to work... he shouldn't wear it when he goes to aunt's, or to the bazaar on his holidays.' In the past year, Ajay showed his dissatisfaction at home for the first time.

'Are you ashamed?' Ramlal made as if he'd pounce on his son and give him a beating. 'Why do you eat the food I bring home by toiling in a chaprasi's uniform? If this shames you, don't live in my house anymore.'

Ajay's eyes had already filled with tears.

'When did I say I was ashamed? I said that because I thought people would say that you don't have anything else to wear. You work and feed Aama, you feed me and my sister, you pay for our school—we see that. My sister and I talk all the time about finishing our education soon and helping you...'

Ajay could say no more. He turned to his mother and burst into loud tears. Narmada was cleaning green beans in the small kitchen; she hunched over and kept at the chore. Mother said—'You scold him needlessly. What wrong has he said? He spoke the truth...'

Chaprasi, who was somewhat dark and thin, with a long nose and fairly large eyes, was tucking the drawstring into the waistband of his suruwal, which he had just finished putting on, as he said, 'I know just what he is saying.'

Thereafter, nothing like this incident occurred in the house for nearly a year. About two months ago, when Ajay was staying home awaiting the results of his final exams, a man wearing a smart tie came to the door, craned in and shouted:

'Is this the chaprasi's home?'

Ajay was on the bed, reading something or another, and he didn't respond even though he had heard the man.

'Is this the chaprasi's home?' the man shouted again.

Ajay got up. He reached the door and kept staring at the man.

'This is it.'

Ajay had said 'this is it' in such a tone that the man became lost for words after hearing it.

'This is it. Why?' Ajay repeated.

'Who are you? The chaprasi's son?' the man asked.

'Yes, I am the chaprasi's son,' Ajay said in the same gruff voice. 'Why? What do you want?'

'It's all right. Nothing,' the man said, turned on his heels, and was gone.

Ajay loathed himself after a while. His mother had started shouting from the kitchen stove, 'People become wiser with study, but your ways will drag us all down a pit someday. The house's man is a chaprasi—the world knows of it. If you don't like that, leave the house and go. We don't want to offend people in our old age on your account. Just let your father return, and see if I don't tell him everything...'

Ajay—perhaps affected by the book he was reading right then—immediately apologized to his mother.

'Get started at a job soon. Everybody will come to show their respect,' Mother said after the rift had been mended.

Now, Ajay had passed his final exams and found a job as an office clerk, and was trying to erase the mark of the chaprasi job from the family name.

Yesterday, he said to his mother, 'Let Babu stop working now.'

Ramlal had started on his job twenty-one years ago, when he had only just become a young man of twenty-one. After spending his first three or four years as chaprasi to the overseer, Ramlal had filled the position that had come to be vacant upon the old man Khatiwada's death, and had thus become chaprasi to the engineer. He had married Pavitra while still working there, and now even his years were fleeing. He had to recognize all sorts of files: which file should be taken to whom; whether or not the file had been examined; if the files had been signed—he had to know everything. Sometimes even the officers couldn't tell which signature belonged to whom: Ramlal had to teach the officers. Contractors would buy tea for the officers to get their bidding done, but it would be the chaprasi who had to run the errand. If Ramlal failed to provide an officer with a loan when asked, it was considered an unofficial inadequacy on his part. Ramlal had suffered many a 'Burra Sahib'. The English engineer he first worked with had been a difficult man. He would make Ramlal run around day and night in a jeep with a red bundle of files. If today was spent in Darjeeling, he'd be in Bakhrakote tomorrow, and the night would be spent at the dak bungalow at Teesta. The son—the same Ajay, barely as big as a fist and perpetually sickly—would be at home. Ramlal had nearly quit his job. But, Ramlal could claim that the district of Darjeeling was built by the same Sahib. There had been an engineer who would leave the office barely once in a month; he would sit in the office and do who knows what—even Ramlal couldn't tell. The present engineer was very smart, he had drawn such awe-inspiring plans that the district would be transformed if everything could be implemented. These days, too, for ten or twelve days each month, Ramlal had to go out on inspections with the Sahib. Who colluded with whom to embezzle how many thousand rupees regarding the landslide at Gorabari before Kharsang; from where did the stone come to build the road to Kalimpong and Algarah and why—Ramlal knew all of this, and more. Ramlal had seen every place, and had grown tired of it all, but he really liked the Baghpul bridge at Subuk, and was never satisfied of standing on the high bridge to watch the green Teesta flow under it.

Upon returning home he would movingly describe Subuk to his wife and children. He would say—Three roads separate there; there the flow of Teesta is imperceptible; the Teesta is very wide, and who knows how deep, who could ever get midstream to measure it? 'If you want to go, come with me. I will talk to the Sahib. Sit quietly in a corner of the jeep and see the sights,' he would say to his son.

Although he'd show excitement about going, Ajay never went. Recently, when a group of drivers took a procession of their vehicles for a picnic, Ajay went together with them and returned after seeing the bridge at Subuk from inside his friend Basanta's Land Rover.

Ajay said to his mother, 'It really is a mesmerizing place, Aama! I will take you there someday.'

Ramlal was drying his red canvas shoes in the sun after washing them and listening to Ajay and his mother. After listening to their talk, he finally said, 'One of the tigers at the northern end of the bridge has been damaged by a rock that fell from the cliff above it. It was an English tiger. It is broken now and the iron rods inside show like ribs. I showed it to the Sahib the other day. It will be rebuilt soon.'

'Let Babu not work anymore.' Two months later, Ajay said this to his mother for the second time.

Mother didn't say anything for a moment.

'We have a lot of loans,' she then said. 'We have three, four hundred rupees to repay. Now that you and your father both have jobs, we will repay the loans.'

'You call that amount a lot of loans?' Ajay twisted his mouth and laughed.

'Your father earns only eighty-seven rupees a month. My plan is to live off that money and shell out your hundred and three to repay the loans over four or five months. After that, we can spend all the money we can, eat what we want, wear what we like... We also need to get you married...'

'Quit this nonsense! Where is it written that Babu should slave away until the day he's thrown from the jeep and breaks his legs?' he asked. 'I will work now. I will take care of everyone. Let him quit his job and stay home. Am I earning one hundred and three rupees for nothing?' Ajay insisted.

'What will your father do at home if he stops working?'

'He will rest,' Ajay said.

Mother had nothing to say in reply.

'Everybody says—there goes the son of a chaprasi, or, that is the daughter of a chaprasi.' Ajay continued, 'Chaprasis at my office call me that. Do we not have other names? When she is called the daughter of a chaprasi, even thieves and illiterate oafs dare look at my sister. They dare shout at you...'

Perhaps his words touched his mother somewhere inwardly; she went inside her room.

That night, Ajay could hear the murmur of his father and mother talking. Ramlal's voice started to climb, until finally he was shouting in the dark.

'So a big babu sahib has been born in this house? Arrogant

prick! I'll drag him out to the street by his hair! I have seen what plenty of babus like you really are. If you are ashamed to be a chaprasi's son, leave my house!'

Ajay crumpled inside his blanket. He had to make an effort even to breathe.

His wife tried to placate him with 'let it be' and 'let it go', but Ramlal continued to rail.

Ajay was still awake until much later, even after the shouting ceased. He was also becoming agitated. He thought—I'll find a job in Calcutta or Assam and leave this place. But he felt love for his sister—and for his sister alone. Narmada wasn't in the habit of complaining. But she must also feel the burn in her heart. And he also found new courage—I shouldn't run away and let Babu's title of chaprasi continue to survive. He recalled the sons of other chaprasis. Only if he could learn what was in their hearts… Ajay spent the night wide awake.

Ramlal protested so much at home, but one day at the office he quietly asked Pradhan, a long-time babu, 'Hajur! I have become old. I can't carry on always being on the road like this. I am thinking of drawing my pension. My son is suggesting the same. In a way, the son will look after the house. He has a job now.'

Pradhan-babu put aside the files he was studying and looked at Ramlal. 'Ramlal, there is no rush. Don't rush, Ramlal—don't you rush!' he said. 'Listen—you and I started working here at the same time. Wait for two more years, and we'll retire together. We had our youth then. We had all sorts of mad fun in this very office. Now we have become old, and the office is getting younger. You have a son, and he has even found a job! But God gave me neither a son, nor a daughter…

But don't you rush! We'll leave this place together, after two years. If you find the work outside difficult, I will keep you as my chaprasi. But stay a while longer. Work here.'

'As you say. I will stay,' said Ramlal.

And now, Ajay would invite many of his friends over and they would come asking for 'Ajay's home'. They would talk about the office, discuss cinema and hockey, and exchange books. Ajay's mother was filled with happiness when they filled her home. When neighbours called it 'Ajay's house', she thought of it as a victory.

Perhaps because of years of habit, or perhaps because of his age, sleep abandoned Ramlal completely by four o'clock in the morning. He would wait for about half an hour for the dawn to show through the window. If he slept in any longer, his back, legs and knees ached. Ramlal would get up. He would start a fire with wood split the night before. As the water boiled in the kettle he would wash with cold water and finish cleaning the house with a broom. He would awake Narmada only after the water had boiled and he had dunked in the little cloth bundle of tea. After finishing a cup he would clean the drains around the house, he would take out the bowls and wash them, wash curtains and towels. He would return at noon to eat.

Ajay's chore was to arrange the books in the house, hang pictures and iron clothes. One day, as he was keeping house, he came across a letter written by Narmada.

'…I am but the unfortunate daughter of a poor chaprasi…,' Narmada had written.

Ajay was afire with rage after reading it.

Two days after this, Basanta's mother and sister came to

the house in search of Narmada. The sister screamed, rousing the village, 'So she has found her mark! The chaprasi's daughter couldn't find anybody else to… She is as dark as Kali to look at. Hey, Kali! Find someone of your own level! It is because you see our wealth, isn't it? You want to live in luxury, do you! If I had a face like that I'd have hanged myself. You won't suit our home. Don't even dream of it!'

Ajay scolded aside his mother and sister and didn't let them shout in reply, and stepped forward.

He had a sharp tongue too. 'Your father owns a jeep now, but we all know what he was like until recently. It isn't that old a story. So, my sister looks like Kali now, does she? You are the prettiest, then. If I had a face like that I would have hanged myself to death. Wonder what hope keeps you alive?'

After a lot more of shouting back and forth, Basanta's elder brother arrived and dragged home the women of his family. He returned later, to talk things through and to apologize.

The apology had the opposite effect on Ajay's mind. His anger, which was directed at the other women until a moment ago, now descended upon his own family. It was because his father had chosen the job of a chaprasi that the family still had to suffer shame and the slings of slights until this day. And now, to erase the stain brought by his sister would take until time itself tired of it…

Ajay scolded his sister first, and then scolded his mother. His father was returning home after a few more days, so he berated him as the source of all misfortune.

The next day, when Ramlal returned for lunch, Ajay's mother said, 'It is enough. You should stop working now. Quit the job.'

Ramlal scrutinized his wife, morsel in hand hanging midway to his mouth.

He continued looking at her, and asked, 'Why?'

'How much longer will you grind your bones?' his wife said. 'You should rest in your old age.'

'And then?'

'Then we'll withdraw money from the fund, sell your pension, and build a decent house. We'll rent a few rooms out. It'll earn the money to provide for us in our old age. It'll be a decent roof over our heads. It will bring prestige.'

'Who gave you these ideas?'

Ajay's mother went quiet. Ramlal continued playing with his rice, but he didn't pick up a morsel.

'Fine, then! We won't say a word more. Do as your heart wants,' after a moment the wife said bitterly.

'So long as my limbs have strength I won't wait for worthless worms to throw me their scraps!' he spoke as if in declaration.

But what would he do after quitting his job? Ramlal had asked himself this question many times before. From that moment he began pondering it more. From the fund and the sale of his pension he might collect seven or eight thousand rupees. That could build a big wooden house. After quitting his job he would sell vegetables at the bazaar. If he could make the rounds of Matigara and Naxal, there would be even more money in it—he thought of it all. After playing with the idea in his mind for two or three days he called Ajay and said, 'A house for five to six thousand rupees, with a bit of a kitchen garden—keep an eye out for it when you are around Haridas Hatta or Rajbari. Don't go asking after it, just keep an eye out for it.'

Ajay immediately nodded a 'yes'.

That night, Ajay spoke to his own heart with some measure of philosophy and also of sentimentality: Rather than rising from clouds to find the sky, the courageous man leaps from the depths of the sea to touch it. Courage is measured by the excess of hardship. Rather than being born into the palace of a king to achieve merely a rung of progress I prefer to attain the heights by starting from the hut of a chaprasi...

In his sleep Ajay saw many shops; he was in need of a lot of milk; he went into many shops and asked for milk but none of the shops had any milk. He was still searching when he woke up.

Not many days had passed before father and son fought again. Five or six people wanting to sell their houses had been found, but because Ramlal didn't show due haste, everybody in the family had become angry, disappointed and despondent. 'Why would the old chaprasi think of our good?' Ajay said before his own mother. And, neither did the mother get angry, nor did she stop him from speaking thus. Ramlal stepped forward to beat his son. The son stood with clenched fists. Ajay didn't hold back his invective. In his rage Ramlal threw the cooked meal of rice and dal onto the street outside.

A throng of onlookers had already gathered. 'They drive their father as if he were a servant,' somebody was saying.

'I am going to kill this selfish creature some day! I'll cut his neck in his sleep!' Ramlal shouted. 'Then I will go to the main bazaar and climb a tall building and shout for everybody to hear, to make everybody listen: "Oh, you unlettered and poor fathers! Never educate your children! Never make that mistake! There is no bigger lie in the world than the lie that our children will study and provide for us…" This is all I will say! I will die only after telling this to the people of Darjeeling!'

Ramlal continued to shout well into the night, nursing a fire. Around two in the morning he perhaps fell asleep for a moment by the hearth. Upon awaking, he continued his muttering. From the noises in the kitchen Ajay guessed that he was making and drinking tea. His heart was also full of hurt; he wished he could ask his father for forgiveness, but something gripped his head and heart and rendered him incapable of it.

Ramlal took his shirts from the chest and tied them in a small bundle. He then folded his blanket atop it.

'I am the one who is not good, the one who isn't right… am I not?' he was saying.

Narmada sat up in her bed and started crying.

Neighbours arrived and began placating Ramlal.

'Don't leave, Babu!' Narmada was crying. Ajay and his mother stood to a side, seeming as if they hoped that the others would manage to stop Ramlal.

'How can you react like this just because the children misbehave? The home always belongs to us, the parents,' Bhaktaman scolded.

After much remonstration, Ramlal stayed.

Ramlal didn't leave, but from that day onwards he felt that he was treated differently at home.

Gradually, the family lost interest in him. Ajay wouldn't speak to him. The immense shame that Ramlal had put in his heart on that day was still raw and unbearable. Ajay's mother would disappear, leaving behind cold rice still sitting over the hearth. His clothes would remain strewn all over the house. Only Narmada would wash his shirts and call him in for meals.

'When I am not around, does your mother talk about me?' Ramlal asked his daughter one day.

'She doesn't,' Narmada said.

'She is ashamed of being a chaprasi's wife. Let her be a big woman and mother to the clerk Ajay,' Ramlal said, perhaps to his daughter, or perhaps to himself.

Narmada stayed silent.

'Fine!' Ramlal said, looking away.

Some three days later, after hurriedly finishing his meal in the morning, Ramlal left home at around nine o'clock. He gave his daughter one rupee to keep, but didn't say anything to anyone else.

A murder of dark crows dipped into and flew from the waters of the Mahanadi river under the Siliguri bridge. Under the Kali temple visible across the river, women bundled together the clothes that had been washed and dried, and gave them to their children to carry as they made their way homewards. But, in the sand that had roasted hot through an afternoon's sun, some half-dozen women and a pair of old men single-mindedly broke stone for construction sites, their gazes undistracted.

Ramlal, who had dragged a sack to sit on and who was watching them, asked the nearest old man, 'Where did you come from?'

'I spent twenty-five years as the chowkidar at the dak bungalow in the Kalimpong forest. I have my pension now. I get eight rupees a month. It is warmer here. I broke gravel on the Teesta until recently. The work there finished, so I came here. It is easier to break the Teesta stone. It is soft, and breaks into even pieces. But the stone of Mahanadi is like heart-stone which even water cannot break. Makes the hammer jump back. See! Like this!'

'Don't you have children? Don't they look after you?' Ramlal suddenly asked.

'I do,' the old man breaking stone said quietly. 'I have a son. He has finished college. But he doesn't earn enough even for himself.'

'It is one thing for a son to treat us as if we're not their fathers, but when our wives treat us as if we aren't their husbands, our hearts break,' Ramlal talked about himself.

A woman who sat breaking stone to a side shouted to a sulky boy in his early teens who was breaking stone without putting any heart into the work, 'Go! Go away! If you'd put your heart into breaking stone we would've finished by now. Go home and start the fire.'

'Your son?' Ramlal asked.

'Yes. Lives with his aunt in Kharsang and goes to the school there. He is home on his holidays. I'd hoped he would help out a little...'

Ramlal called the boy to him and said, 'Bring ten cups of tea for all of us. Bring two big loaves of bread, too.' Ramlal gave him a five-rupee note.

The next afternoon, Ramlal was walking alone across the Baghpul bridge at Subuk. He paused in the middle and looked down through the strong English rails.

The Teesta flowed inaudibly, green and deep. So much

water! Leaves swept up by the wind from the jungle around it fell into the water and quietly flowed downstream. How immense was the Teesta! How patient and tranquil! It gave succour to those who gazed at it. It could sweep away everything along its banks if it so decided, but it had determined not to do so. The heart swelled with so much joy just to look at it. He dropped all the money in his pocket to the water below. The wind didn't let the coins drop straight, and swept them farther out over the river. All the coins made fleeting white spots on the green, flowing water. He took the rope out from his pocket and dropped it into the water. A new rope stretched slowly on the surface, then coiled into itself and was lost into the water, and again showed itself for a flash before disappearing. Now he possessed nothing. He discarded the coat. It tumbled with the force of the wind and landed upturned on the water, exposing its torn lining, and made as if to raise itself from the river. Somewhere in Ramlal's heart was the forceful pounding of sorrow. But he really did also feel the joy of dying in the Teesta. He climbed onto the rails and said his final prayer. 'Do not let me die as I fall, Teesta! Let me die in your waters.'

Ramlal's corpse emerged two miles downstream, by the gates of a village. Ajay took people from Darjeeling and returned after cremating the corpse where it had been found.

On that day, he wrote in his diary: 'We were ashamed as long as he lived. He brought everlasting shame upon us by dying in this manner.'

And, as if agreeing with the sentiment, his mother didn't even shed a tear.

The Delinquent

I have been wanting to write many stories about the boys whom I taught. More so than students who find jobs in offices or teach at schools, I have more affection for those who find other vocations and become drivers, or clerks at tea gardens, or even run tea shops—a student has a beautiful shop on the sloping road at Poshak. While in school, they see us as men of courage and ideals; and, as teachers, we take it as our duty to impress it upon them, and to influence them through the lives we live. Here I am writing a story of one of my students—Padam.

Padam left high school after failing his ninth grade. I will never forget how he made me laugh on the day the examination results were published. Even in the swarm of boys milling in the schoolyard, he stood aloof, wearing a dejected face. He smiled a little upon seeing me.

'What are your results?' I asked.

'Rotten, sir,' he said. He was a well-built lad, fair of face. He wore a loosely knit yellow cardigan.

'What went bad?' I asked again.

'English.'

Padam wasn't the kind to pass English. Let alone analysis, he would get even the narration wrong. During my classes, I would move him from his seat by the window to the benches in the front of the class.

'Only that?' I asked.

'And Maths.'

'And?'

'Sanskrit.'

'And also?'

'History.'

'So you failed everything?'

He stood in shame.

I was pondering what he should do next when he volunteered, 'Sir, I won't study any more.'

The winter holidays started that day, and through that winter I worked on completing my novel *Aaja Ramita Chha*. In my determination to write a chapter each day, I forgot all about Padam's problems. My winter, from mid-December to mid-February, was spent under a quilt amid sheets of paper. School started again. I returned much thinner. A new year began among new students and students who had returned renewed. Like a handful of other boys who had been lost, I inquired about Padam, but nobody had a satisfactory answer for me.

It must have been the month of April or May when, during the third period, as I was teaching grammar to the ninth graders, I saw Padam arrive and stand outside the door. Some twenty minutes later, when I came out of the classroom after finishing the lesson, Padam stood at a distance, still waiting for me. I felt a particular joy upon seeing him—as if reunited with an estranged younger brother.

'What is it, Padam?' I asked.

In his hands folded in a namaste he held a notebook, and folded in it were some papers.

'I wanted to trouble you for something, sir,' he said humbly and unfolded the papers. They were a couple of forms for a lottery from Uttar Pradesh; all tickets gone, sold by Padam. He had come to ask help with sending the money through postal orders and to get a letter written. I felt happy, and also tender. 'Where did you find so many people?' I asked with genuine surprise. 'My own neighbours from the tea garden. Only one is an outsider,' he said, affected by my praise.

'How much do you make for selling two books of tickets?' I asked him again. Padam laughed and said, 'I get twelve rupees, sir.' If he earns that amount every month, he will be spared his grandmother's nagging, I surmised. I bought him postal orders during the tiffin break, wrote out all of them, cross-checked them, and finally wrote a letter and put all the papers in a registered envelope.

'A ticket for you, sir,' Padam took out the forms from the envelope, and he really had left one of the last tickets for me. Seeing no way out, I took the ticket and asked, 'How many thousands for the first prize?'

'The first prize is a lakh rupees, sir.' He spoke with hope and confidence. 'If you win the first prize, sir, we who sold it to you also get twelve thousand rupees.'

'You will someday earn that much money even if you never win a lottery,' I said to Padam.

The next month, he had similarly sold four entire lottery books. He was feeling accomplished at being able to show his achievement. And, just like the time before, there was a last ticket waiting for me again.

'Never make anybody work without pay,' I must have taught his class at some point, in a particular context. I suspected if this lottery ticket wasn't a result of that.

But Padam didn't return after this second visit. Many months passed, and I assured myself that he had found a job at a tea garden somewhere.

Early one day he came to my home in a panic. I had heard the night before that the Madhisey cowherds from the plains—to whom I had given space on my fields to build and live in a shed—had cut down the alder trees at the far end of the field. I was about to go and check when Padam arrived. The Assam Rifles were recruiting, and he, too, wanted to enroll. In a frenzied rush I acquisitioned his school certificate and wrote out a character certificate for him, and accompanied him to the Employment Exchange. He had grown taller than me, robust of body; Padam was recruited without hassle.

'I had a student named Padam. This is how his story ended,' I told myself while returning home and sighed with satisfaction, but little did I know that his story actually began on that very day.

Whenever I met Nepalis coming from Assam, I would ask about the Assam Rifles and, with anybody who could elaborate even a little, I would enquire about Padam.

'He is making good progress there,' somebody from the Rifles told me one day.

'He doesn't write to me,' I unthinkingly blurted out a complaint.

'He has become a strapping lad with the Rifles' training,' this was all the man added to the news before parting ways—I must have met him at the cinema.

I heard after many more months that he beat up his own captain while playing hockey, made the man's face swell up, was imprisoned in the barracks, and that he had now become a delinquent, shirking his duties, bickering with his officers and refusing to do any work.

I thought—he wouldn't do that if he didn't feel more than a little bit bullied.

I heard later that Padam had left the Rifles and worked with the National Cadet Corps somewhere in Manipur.

So, he had found some form of employment. I felt satisfied.

I had a moment of panic last year, sometime around July. Confidential papers arrived from Mandalay in Burma, asking me about Padam. The moment I started reading the papers, my heart told me that he must be in some sort of trouble. I wrote—and got written—good things to the best of my knowledge, and the best I could manufacture about him, and dispatched a registered letter the very next day. But my heart was still full of trepidation. A month passed, and another, but nothing more came of it.

But Krishna Prasadji in Manipur had written back aplenty in response to my queries. He said Padam had started the 'Darjeeling Hotel' there. It seems to be doing very well, he had written. But there was no news beyond that.

If I were concerned with pursuing just one issue, I could give it my full attention. Events descend upon me in sudden waves.

On a Saturday, I had gone to the Nepali Sahitya Parishad to chat with my friends when a Madhisey chaprasi in a khaki uniform came searching for me.

'Are you I.B. Sir?' he asked in rustic Hindi.

'Yes. What is it?' I asked, not bothering to get up.

In broken Hindi, he said, 'I went to your home, searching everywhere, a man on the road told me you were in the school. When I reached the school, the chowkidar said you were at a municipal meeting, there the secretary sahib said go to the Sahitya Parishad. Now, where was the Sahitya Parishad...'

'What's the matter?' I said. I still did not understand what he was getting at after such a longwinded approach.

'This Sahib sends you his greetings,' he said and handed me a white card. It read 'P. Nepali' in English. I couldn't imagine it meant Padam.

'Where is he staying?' I asked.

'At the new hotel. Look at the back of the card.'

Indeed, on the reverse of the card was the address for Hotel Mount Everest, room number 46. My teacher's instinct checked if 'Everest' had been misspelt. The letters were like the scratching of hens; I couldn't discern a misspelling. I remembered making the class laugh by once calling it 'hen-writing'.

'Hello, sir!' He extended his hand when he saw me after opening the wooden door to his room. I did not take his hand. He immediately joined his hands in namaste.

'Namaste, sir! Did you recognize me?'

'Namaste! You are Padam,' I said.

He was guiding me to the grand hall. Chequered suit, a tie, pointed, polished black shoes. 'Where did you find the money?' I felt like abruptly asking him.

Even after reaching the hall, he continued to walk and talk. I sat on a couch with cushions. He spoke, standing up,

'Am very busy sir. Just for two days, just to meet you sir, I came to Darjeeling. Will fly directly to Kolkata and fly back day after to Ceylon. Have no time.'

'Ceylon is Sri Lanka. Say—Shillong.' I said with the intention of deflating him.

'Have started a big hotel in Manipur sir. You, madam, everyone—let's go tomorrow. What is left in your job, anyway?'

He called a waiter and ordered coffee for both of us.

I asked, 'What happened to you in Burma?'

'Got into trouble sir, but survived because of your letter and a letter from the NCO at Guwahati. Got arrested in Kalaura. Had entered without a passport.'

'And why were you there?' The coffee tasted strange, so I said this with a grimace.

'To do business.' He finished his cup and looked at me. 'If I am to do business… my eyes have opened now.'

While walking towards Chowrasta, I said to him, 'Come, let's go home. Eat with us before you leave.'

'I still remember the taste of your cooking sir, but I can't come today. Have no time. I only came to take you to Manipur. I still insist sir, come with me. I have nobody to look after all that business. After all, I have nobody of my own.'

We entered P. C. Banerjee's shop on the way; I went in because he had entered the shop. He bought a women's watch worth more than 300 rupees, gave me the box, and said, 'Present for madam.'

I had already become cautious so I said, 'She already has a watch. What would she do with this one? Wear a watch each on either wrist?'

'Please choose something else, then.'

I considered and said, 'No need.'

Padam's face became dark and full of hurt. It was as if it were evidence that he really did revere me.

'They said you were about to publish a novel. I heard you even read out excerpts. Was it published?' he asked momentarily, full of hope.

'A collection of short stories is also being published,' I said.

'Sir, how much will you need?' Padam opened the zipper on the bag hanging from his hand and looked at me. The large bag was full of currency notes.

'No need—somebody else is publishing it,' I said. 'It is writing that bleeds you dry; publishing is nothing difficult.'

Padam nearly wept right there.

But even I couldn't be any more cruel than that, so I said, 'Send me a camera later.'

'Buy a Rolliflex sir, or buy a Yashica.' He grinned with joy and shoved an entire bundle of cash into my pocket. 'You can get one for a hundred and fifty rupees in Burma. Everything is cheap there.' He sought to flee. 'I have to go, sir. Please give madam my regards, and please wire if you are coming to Manipur. I have to go. Namaste.' Padam rushed away.

Not a whole year has passed since and Padam has returned to my home. He is in the next room, with the others, making selroti for Tihar. I cannot refrain from writing down the story that he just told me. But I should only write factual descriptions; I will not touch upon the 'truth' in them. If I smother it with my perspective, and if I confine it within meanings that I provide, it will not remain the story that Padam experienced. I don't want to be bogged down in a story today in the name of empathy.

'Why did you quit the NCC job?' I had asked Padam earlier.

'When I was working with the NCC in Manipur, there was a Lushei tribal named Yashu,' Padam said. 'He'd always come to me and say, "Pshaw! Why would you keep your job? What's there in it? Two hundred rupees a month at most. I can earn that two hundred in one minute." And, in truth, he always had a bag full of money. He'd get drunk, crumple up new notes and scatter them. I had to pick them up and keep them. Whenever I got off work, he showed up at two in the afternoon, took me to the cinema or sightseeing, dined me, spent his money like anything. And, while conducting parades I also thought—this is a worthless job! A hundred and eighty six rupees for the entire month! I don't want this damned job! And so I quit.'

'Did you then open the Darjeeling Hotel?' I asked.

'And the hotel did so well!' Padam, who now looked pale and thin, said with astonishment. 'There were more than sixty of just college students who kept a regular tab for their meals. And, everything was so cheap in Manipur. Nearly hundred and fifty chickens were butchered each day. Never kept account of butter and eggs. I made seven thousand rupees in just three months. If I had continued running the hotel, I would have a lakh rupees now.'

I was a little fed up of this talk of thousands and lakhs. 'And you quit that?' I asked him.

'But all of this was bound to happen,' Padam said to himself instead of replying to my question.

'What trade did you take up then?' I repeated.

'Smuggling marijuana, selling it in the black market,' Padam said.

Marijuana! Black market! I must have shouted—where did you find such company?

Padam smiled a little. Didn't speak for a moment. 'They'd come to the hotel. Many businessmen.' Padam continued to relate his story. 'They'd come, stay at the hotel. Eight, ten of them would shut themselves in a room on the top floor and play cards all day long. Would chat with me. When I listened, I realized that some of them were smugglers of opium and marijuana. They carried bags of money, arranged in stacks, tied with red rubber bands. When they said, "You just need a little bit of courage to make it rain cash," I thought they were saying that to me. There was one who smuggled goods from Burma into India. I left somebody else in charge of the hotel and went with him into Burma.'

'Without a passport,' I reminded him.

'Got arrested in Kalaura.'

I had told myself that I would look up Kalaura on the map, but it appears I forgot.

'Many Burmese, Gorkhalis and Assamese travel back and forth here. I don't know just how they got to me! I was detained for two months. Later, they were very nice about letting me go. Not only did they release me, I got a six-month permit to travel through Burma after spending just a hundred rupees.

'I reached Mandalay within eight days of being released. A man only needs courage. God has indeed made this world for man to enjoy. I had a reference in Mandalay so I straight away went to Jasraj Rai. The old man had once been a Lieutenant Major. What a splendid life that man lives. I had about twenty-five thousand rupees on me. And everything is so much cheaper in Burma. A Relay bicycle that costs four hundred rupees here is just one…'

'Not Relay—Raleigh!' I corrected.

'Seven O'Clock razors were two paisa apiece. Roamer watches were sixty rupees. I bought as much as I could and stored everything at the old man's. The old man's men had the job of taking everything across the border. I was living it up there while the goods made it to Garo Hills here. My job was to spend money all day and...'

'And get drunk?' I asked.

'No, sir. The Lieutenant Major has a daughter,' Padam said and became quiet.

'What about her?' I tried to give him the chance to overcome his shyness. 'My job was to drive around in the old man's jeep all day with that daughter. I adored even the way Latika wore the Burmese dress. Did not know Nepali, spoke a bit of Hindi, but mostly just Burmese talk.'

It was a deep blow that he had suffered. Knowing that, I changed the topic.

'Did you reach Manipur safely?'

'With that fifteen thousand sir, I had earned fifty or sixty thousand rupees. I had taken to heart that I would go and settle in Burma. I had been teaching Latika a bit of Nepali in the six weeks of my stay there. If you had agreed then to look after my hotel in Manipur, I would have by now...'

I too felt my conscience prickle.

'After returning from here, I went to Calcutta. From there, I went to Silchar with marijuana. There is an old grandmother who lives on Elgin Road in Calcutta, at the far corner of the Shambhunath Hospital. I had bought four large water jars to carry marijuana. I went to the grandmother's to seal the jars with shellac wax. I stayed at the Grand Hotel, but in this line of work, I had to store the goods at a different hotel under a different name. In the night, I packed the jars tight with marijuana and sealed them. After sealing them I poured a bit of water into each jar: I was bringing back Ganga water from Brindaban.'

Padam had a good laugh. 'If anybody had asked?' He would mutter a few phrases, he said, in Assamese and Lushei.

'Everybody got inspected at Pandughat. Nobody checked me. Four jars of marijuana—through! Once we reached the other side on the jeep, all the Assamese kept nagging me for Ganga water. They'd come with bowls and bottles in their hands. I lied to them for no good, I thought. Only after I stood up and shouted at them did they stop asking me for Ganga water.'

'How much did you make?' I asked.

'Seventeen hundred was the rate,' he explained. I didn't understand.

'The second time, I smuggled marijuana from Biratnagar. I stayed below at Jogbani. A merchant arranged the deal. When I reached Badabazaar in Calcutta with three maunds of contraband the merchant's jaws dropped. Apparently nobody had managed to get more than a maund at a time before that. I went there with three whole maunds of it. You don't deal in cheques in this business. My hands tired from hauling around a bag of cash the entire night.'

Then he addressed himself just as much as he addressed me—'But, in this line of work, everybody gets caught after two or three trips.' He had become a particular stripe of a superstitious man. But, in that moment, I couldn't counter that superstition either.

'For the last time, I took marijuana from Sylhet to Calcutta. I spent all of my capital to bring twelve maunds of weed. Packaging in rubber-paper started a week early. Soaked the weed in milk and packed it. I found the hotel a nuisance and had already sold it; sold it for cheap, too. I would get scared. I told myself many times, "This is the last time I do this—this is my last time. I won't keep up this treacherous trade."

'The stuff got nabbed before reaching Calcutta.' Padam had become incapable of showing any emotion or even comprehension.

'I got away by claiming that the goods weren't mine, but it was a death blow!' Padam managed to wring out these words.

'It seems I made a futile escape on an aeroplane. Reached Shivsagar, Lakhimpur... then reached Biratnagar. When I saw dark and pale marijuana plants standing two feet tall in the farms I felt like embracing them and weeping with them, crying with them. I felt I would get something back. I stood there and cried, watching the plants. Then I found myself in Kharsang. Only then did I come to my senses.

'But... I don't know why, but I went to Manipur again. Reached there after dark. I ran into an old man from Khumoi whose life had been ruined after he was caught and jailed for being in the same line of work. He had already heard the news about me. "In this line," he said, peering at me through his drooping eyelids, "In this line you don't get caught the first time or the second time—you get caught the third time. I got caught on my third trip; Chital got caught; Harip got caught. Everybody gets caught the third time..."

'It was only then that I understood how utterly devastated I had become.'

After saying this, Padam even stopped rubbing vegetable shortening into the rice flour. I heard a quiet, sobbing hiccup escape from his chest.

I said with the intention of providing him with something to aspire towards, 'You lost a turn, you haven't lost your entire life. You'll reach Burma again someday, you'll meet that girl, and you can elope with her to Garo Hills.'

'What do I have to show for myself in Mandalay?' Padam asked me. 'There are better-looking men working as drivers at her place. Men better educated than me work as clerks for the Lieutenant Major. Back then I had money, which I don't have any of anymore.'

I remembered Padam asking for two rupees in the morning.

'Padam—don't get distracted any longer. Think of the past as a nightmare and forget everything. I will find you a job in a shop somewhere. Earn a living through a job, just like the rest of us.'

'Pshaw! What's there in a job!' he immediately said and, oblivious of the rest of us, became lost in his thoughts.

In Limbo

Now the girl's father spoke with great restraint and severe effort.

'I'm meeting so many of you, from far-flung corners, here, today—and such gentlefolk, too—because of this girl—she is my chhori, my eldest daughter. It is a good thing to make each other's acquaintance, there is no harm in it, but to meet for the first time under circumstances like this is ill met. But we have to somehow make arrangements for these two—this girl, and this boy, my jwain. I have accepted him as my son-in-law—since my daughter has already spent ten whole days in this house I have no choice but to accept him as my son-in-law—and we have to arrange for them to spend their lives together.

'Perhaps I have erred in saying that to meet under circumstances like this is ill met, and for that I beg your forgiveness. Neither have I travelled here today to speak so rudely. Among us Nepalis, a girl's father never goes about searching for his son-in-law's home. But I have put aside my honour and pride, and I have come to the man's house like a dog. The reason—my love for this girl. Perhaps you have daughters and sisters, too. There is the proverb—which our elders surely forged from experience and knowledge—the needle in the corner eventually moves to the middle of the room. Perhaps some of you have been in a similar plight before, or perhaps you will go through something like this in future, because this thing called a daughter, it seems to me, is nothing but a hive of worries and blame.

'On Wednesday of the week before, my sister-in-law's husband called me at the office, down at the Pankhabari Tea Estate, and gave me the news—"Kumari hasn't been home since yesterday. I hear she has eloped, with a Gurung boy of our community. Your sister-in-law finally gave me the news this morning. She didn't even tell me the evening before. I thought she was home, so I didn't ask after her, because she usually always stayed in. But daughters do leave the home one day, after all..." When I heard the news, it made me somewhat glad, but also a bit sad. "Is this why you took Kumari up to Darjeeling?" I scolded him. Then I became angry with myself. Kumari had become upset with me over something trivial and left the estate to go and live with her aunt. Every event since that incident must have neatly fallen into order to arrive at this accident.

'But I am a father, and my heart worried. On the morning of the third day, I left Pankhabari and arrived here at Kumari's aunt's. The Gurungs and the Chhetris have mixed from a long ago, and there is no tradition among us Chhetris to take back our daughters who have eloped. My daughter will live as her fate keeps her. But look at us—for three whole days we didn't get even a word about her! We felt very humiliated, but we swallowed our anger—if we were to go to the police and the

courts, she would still be our daughter, and he our son-in-law.
I kept berating my sister-in-law. I said, "How could you have
so blindly let her go with a Gurung savage?" It has been some
days since the estate has buzzed with gossip—that the head
clerk Raya-babu's eldest daughter is married now, and that
she eloped with a college-educated boy. Here, before you, I
am a simpleton from the tea estates, a hick who doesn't know
how to speak, an idiot who forgets everything he had thought
he would say to you. But back at the estate, I have esteem; I
enjoy quite a bit of respect and, because of the respect I have
earned, this motherless girl also had respect. When I didn't
hear any news for three days—again, mine is a father's heart—I
started imagining all sorts of things, I started worrying about
this and that. What if they don't like my daughter? What if
they throw her out of their house? My mind and heart were
smothered under anxiety. And, as you can see here, it was just
as I thought it would be.

'When, after eight whole days, nothing was heard from
the boy's side, I arrived in Darjeeling early in the morning
yesterday. It is a tea estate owned by Bengalis and, as you
know well, it is impossible to get even a day off. But I came.
When I saw that my daughter's whole life was in disarray, I
came to make arrangements. When I got here, I asked my
nephew if he knew jwain's house here and he said, "I know
it." Then I told him to hurry and take a letter to his cousin.
I hadn't written anything much to my daughter in the letter.
Perhaps jwain's father has kept the letter—you can ask him
for it and read it. I had said, "Between six and nine in the
evening, come to your aunt and uncle's home, just you and
your husband. You don't have to bring anything. I'll give you

both tika and bless you."That was all I had written. We waited through the evening. We prepared whatever food we had at home, and we waited for them. Eight o'clock, and then nine o'clock, and still they didn't arrive and I went outside and walked around to check; whenever someone approached down the road I would imagine it was them. I'd worry that it would be embarrassing to be seen out in the yard, waiting for them, so I'd hurry into the house. And it was nine o'clock, then ten, and eventually it was midnight. I cried alone that night. A man doesn't cry in pain or fear, but he cries out of shame.

'I was returning to the estate by bus at eight o'clock in the morning today. Everybody accused me of fleeing to the estate. The bus was taking me away, but my heart kept running back to this place. When our bus reached Ghoom, when more people climbed on board, I was startled. Let it be, my daughter's life and happiness are bigger than my honour, I thought, and I got off the bus. The bus fare, already paid until Kharsang, went to waste. I caught a jeep coming in this direction and returned here. Here I am now, standing before you like a dog.

'Jwain's mother just now explained that the delay yesterday was because you had to wait for jwain's elderly uncle, and I accept that. You couldn't come yesterday, and that is all right, because I then had to come here myself, and now we have become acquainted. I am sure yesterday's humiliation and sadness hasn't made me weaker; I have forgotten that thought too. And now I have seen jwain; he is of the gentlemanly type, and I am happy, not just outwardly, but I am very happy on the inside. I have seen your home, and I have already told my daughter that her life will be spent well in a household like this. You have shown me hospitality. You were all also singing and dancing in the room outside. Everybody believed that a wedding was taking place. It was only in the hearts of the family members here, in the depths of my heart, and in the tears in this girl's eyes that the truth was known.

'I had said that I wanted to bless the bride and groom with tika. You barred my hand. You said that jwain's uncle had died this year, and that tika wouldn't be possible. The reason you give is correct—a death in the family does bar tika through the following year. But if that was the case, why was jwain's mother in such a hurry to bring her daughter-in-law home? Not only did she send other women to talk to chhori, she herself went three or four times to fetch her. If you had waited, you would have earned the time to get to know the girl better, and all of this would have happened only after the boy had also come to like her. Now, it must be as if you can neither swallow nor spit out what you have chewed off. As for me—I am in no place to either take her home with me, or leave her here. I took her mother's honour as my own, and kept it intact even after her death. But now I see the daughter, whom I raised with all my love and affection, is about to be discarded like rubbish. Chhori, it is because you carried your destiny in your own hands, according to your own wishes, that your fate is now like that of a dirty scrap of paper. If you had trusted your father with it, you wouldn't have been in this plight.

'I had come here imagining that I would get the paperwork made for the boy and the girl and take it with me. But I see now that it will be impossible. I have seen many homes that couldn't stay together despite having papers. Now I know

how immature my faith was, and how it has let me down.
Chhori, I knew your mother's heart, and I can understand
your worry. Don't you cry! I understand how much meaning
and importance the prospect of spending your life with your
husband holds for you right now. You are crying because you
are also afraid. And it seems you have also started feeling love
for jwain. Earlier, I saw you and jwain talking in your room. It
is possible that somebody else in the house dislikes you, that
they have heard something bad about you, and maybe even
your husband cannot defy that person's wishes. And perhaps
there really is something bad about you—maybe I'm the only
one who doesn't know it.

'My heart told me to take the two of you to your aunt
and uncle's place. The two of you immediately agreed. And
I saw that you had come before me in a newly bought sari.
Jwain was also wearing a new green suit. But I don't know
what jwain's mother told him inside, because I don't see him
anywhere anymore. And now you stand here, in your new
sari, crying alone by my side.

'All I had wanted was for the two of you to go and meet
your aunt and uncle. I had hoped to talk to jwain in the
meanwhile, explain a few things to him. My jwain, who is
more educated than I am and who earns more than I do—
there was no way I could turn him against his family and
bring him over to my side in just one day. "Her father is here,
after all. We can meet the other relatives later," jwain's mother
said earlier. My heart is brimming with suspicion, but there
is nothing I dare to speak out aloud.

'It doesn't suit me to come here and sit like this in your
home for hours on end. But I can't leave this daughter of

mine in limbo like this either. Please, let us have you tell me if I should take this girl back. Chhori, don't cry now! Or, all of you tell me what you have decided. All I want is for you to give me an answer.

'Earlier, jwain's mother came to me and said, "We brought our daughter-in-law home, and we aren't asking for her to leave. Let her stay in this house for as long as she wants. We won't tell her not to."

'And, that is all well said, but still, I don't know why, from deep inside, my heart just can't accept this…'

We Separated Them

Yesterday evening, I had gone to the panchayat as a supporter from the husband's side. Although I do not know Bhaktiman very well, I hadn't been able to refuse him when he came in the morning to say, 'You'll have to come with me in the evening, okay?'

She arrived when called forth after everybody had settled down at the panchayat—her four-year-old son walking before her, head covered with the short end of a pale sari—and sat on the opposite bench. The son must have spotted Bhaktiman as he walked in front of his mother because, before the mother could do anything about it, he came running to his father, shouting, 'Baba! Baba!' Bhaktiman picked his son up and put him on his lap. 'Why haven't you come home, Baba? Where had you gone, Baba?' The child began asking, loudly enough for everybody in the hall to hear. I can never watch such a scene; my heart soured with sadness. I looked at Bhaktiman's wife—apparently, I had never seen her before. She was perhaps twenty-three or twenty-four, thin, bright of face, even pretty. Even now she wore sindoor in the parting of her hair. It became visible because the sari had slipped from her head and fallen to her shoulder. She covered her head once more with the end of her sari. She glanced at Bhaktiman once, then turned to look at us and smiled.

'What sort of a woman is this!' I elbowed Bal Bahadur and said, 'Look how she smiles at us!'

Bal Bahadur replied, 'Slut! She's a slut!'

I didn't look in her direction again.

'We must begin the panchayat now,' the sarpanch, revered among the villagers, said. 'You, the panchas, know very well that the panchayat met a week ago, right here at the school hall, to discuss the complaints brought by Bhaktiman against his wife Laxmi. He showed many reasons and brought forth accusations against his wife so that he may separate from her. The panchayat couldn't deliver a sound decision on that day. Because it was necessary for us to carefully deliberate over various issues. Our secretary will read out all of this to you now.'

From the panchayat's register a college-going young man read out all the decisions from the previous meeting of the panchayat: Laxmi to stay for a week with a friend; Bhaktiman to provide her with seven rupees to cover the cost of her upkeep for the week; in the interim, the secretary to write to Laxmi's parents at Nine Mile in Kalimpong and summon them; and, in the meanwhile, the president of the committee to go to Bhaktiman's neighbourhood and make necessary inquiries.

From the secretary we heard that Laxmi's father had received the letter, but he had neither replied, nor had he deigned to appear in person.

'You tell us first, Bhaktiman,' the sarpanch said. 'Why do you ask to be separated? Why don't you ask to live with your wife, share the good and the ill, make a home and live with love? And, your son's future—do you two wish to, you know, to ruin it?'

After asking these questions the elder looked at all of us.

Bhaktiman stood up, sat his son where he had been sitting, and faced the panchas to speak.

'Sanad! Come here!' Laxmi scolded her son.

'Why don't *you* come here?' the son teased.

'Brat!' she said and laughed.

Even the people sitting behind us commented, 'This woman must have a screw loose in her head. Look at how she laughs!'

Bhaktiman said, 'Earlier, I had employed Laxmi to cook and clean for me. Before that, she used to work at somebody else's home. When she was with me for about a year and half, I observed her ways, her habits and behaviour, how she did her chores. I inquired about her parents, about her home. This girl comes from a very poor family. One day, I said to her, "It seems you have been through a lot of hardship. I have nobody to call my own either. Let us live as husband and wife. You'll have a bit more comfort, and my life will find a purpose." I had thought—this girl has grown up in destitution; if she gets even just a bit more of comfort, it will be enough. Laxmi said, "I'll have to ask my father." I said, "Very well. Ask him." When the letter reached them, both the father and the mother came. Then, we invited a handful of people from the neighbourhood, served them tea and puris, sweets. Call it the wedding or the wedding feast, that was all that ever happened.

'Then, this son was born. Everything was going smoothly. If she set her heart on something, I did whatever it took to find the money to buy what she wanted. I continued to work at the book shop—I still do. But, her heart was going astray…'

It seemed Bhaktiman was having trouble speaking anymore. I stared at the floor, lost in my thoughts. 'Go on, tell us everything. You must tell the panchas everything clearly,' the sarpanch said.

'I spend all of my days at the shop. It seems all sorts or strangers were frequenting my home. When I heard this from my neighbours, I died of shame. Even I chanced upon a few young men, sitting in my home. One of them I know very well—he is a thief who has been to the jail many times. When I asked, she said—They are people I met here and there, a long time ago. I talked to her, I scolded her, I tried everything. But she attacked me instead. Not a day goes by without a fight anymore. Our neighbours have grown tired of listening to us fight. I don't get to drink tea in the morning; when I get home in the evening, she and the son will have already eaten and gone to bed. There is nothing left out for me. God is my witness—I have gone to bed on an empty stomach for four straight nights…'

'Did you sleep hungry, or did my son and I sleep hungry? Liar!' Laxmi shouted fierily to interrupt.

'No, no! You may not scream like this at the panchayat. Speak only when we ask you to,' one of the panchas scolded her.

'But, how can he tell lies?' Laxmi shouted again. 'Lying bully!'

'Listen, Nani,' the sarpanch said. 'You are as a daughter to us, but the manner in which you are speaking to your husband—that is not good. If this is how you behave towards your husband here, before so many respected people, how must you treat him when you are alone! That is what we have heard from your neighbours, too. Tell me—didn't the neighbours come to your home five or six months ago and hold a panchayat there to reconcile the two of you?'

'I have already explained my plight before the panchas. Please, just think—how can I live with her after all of this?' Bhaktiman sat down.

'Leave out the small stuff, but explain your case clearly before the panchas,' the sarpanch ordered Laxmi. 'Has your husband given you trouble, or has he gone astray with other women? What is it? Tell the panchas everything clearly. You can speak from where you are standing.'

'Whatever I say, I'll speak the truth,' Laxmi began. 'He has the terrible habit of envious eyes. He has already accused me with everyone in the neighbourhood. If you keep house, people will visit. But whenever anybody comes for a visit, he says, "That is your lover! Get lost with him!" He makes a scene. He has made it impossible for me to keep face in the village. The sacrifices I have made to make this house into a home, not buying the food my heart wanted, not going to the cinema—if he weren't totally blind, he would have seen it. He gives ten rupees for the entire week. With that I have to buy food, and then clothes and utensils for the house...'

'I've been buying her extra clothes,' Bhaktiman stood to speak.

'You won't speak now,' a pancha stopped him.

'Don't speak, not now,' I also said.

'During the wedding, he had promised that he would look after my parents. Maybe he gave them ten rupees once, but after that he hasn't given them anything. I bought and gathered everything there is in the house now. He doesn't even give me money to run the household anymore. What does he expect me to cook for him then? When he is at the shop, he orders tea and snacks and eats it with his friends there. Fine, I was at home, going to bed hungry. But when this little boy also had to go to bed hungry, I went to the shop one day to ask for money. He attacked me at the shop, tried to beat me, and said, "Why have you come to the shop?" I shouted at him then, out of anger. It was that night that four of five of these people held a panchayat.'

'Are you talking about something old, or something that happened recently?' one of the panchas asked.

'After the panchayat reconciled us, things were good for a few days, but became the same after that,' she said.

Members of the panchayat had begun their cross-questioning and interrogation. Ambar, Bal Bahadur and I went outside to smoke cigarettes.

'Where is this girl from?' I asked Ambar after lighting my cigarette and using the same match to light his.

'Kalimpong,' Ambar inhaled deeply, then exhaled three times. 'I know this poor girl from a while ago.'

This is what I gathered from what Ambar told:

The father was poor as a wild-bee; the air, the rain, the sun, the wind, all had free passage into the house. Poverty had opened the eyes of Laxmi's heart and mind early. When she was eleven, Laxmi left her home to work at Dhan Bahadur Mandal's. There she saw Mandal's home, filled with a thousand treasures of bowls and cauldrons, pots and vases, lamps and boxes and beds. Laxmi would happily stay there, even without pay, to sit and walk and work among all the splendour. She would wish—If only our home were like this! When Mandal's wife ordered the servants about from the upper floor, giving them a thousand tasks, Laxmi would stand enrapt in a corner and watch.

When she grew up and started carding wool at the godown under Homes, her co-worker women, young and middle-aged alike, would talk racily, tease and laugh. But Laxmi would only listen quietly. She never thought of whether her husband ought to be of this sort or that sort. Rather, she dreamed of having a house, full to the brim with stuff and more goods of all sorts. Day and night Laxmi dreamed of a yard alive with hens and ducks, children frolicking before the house, the house filled with clothes and quilts and blankets, the kitchen adazzle with wine glasses and polished brass plates, an endless throng of visitors calling and taking their leave.

Perhaps many of the wishes in Laxmi's heart were fulfilled while she lived as Bhaktiman's wife. Compared to her parents' house, this house was a thousand times better appointed. And, even if she had to eat cheap, Laxmi was desperate to gather goods for her home. In her heart, there was the pride and joy and pleasure of possessing things that she had never imagined of owning in many lives to come. Well, let the world see her possessions, too! Whenever she ran into somebody from her old life in the bazaar, she insisted upon inviting them home. And she invited many more people besides. And, so many simply jumped at any excuse to visit.

When we went inside again, a pancha was asking Laxmi, 'Are you willing to be separated, or no?'

'If he is ready to separate, I am also ready to separate.'

'Don't say, "If he is ready,"' the pancha said. 'Speak for yourself. Do you, in your heart, wish to separate, or no?'

About then, I stood to say, 'I have a humble request before

the learned gentlemen of the panchayat. The priority of the panchayat ought to be to create reconciliation, something a court is incapable of doing. Only if such efforts come to nothing should it resort to the unwelcome task of separation. In my humble opinion, my friend and his wife should be given one more opportunity through the panchayat to reconcile and steer forth the raft that is family. Instead of asking whether they are prepared to separate, perhaps we should ask them—"Are you ready to reconcile?"'

Laxmi had been watching my face, and finding hope and courage, she continued to look the others in their faces. I continued to speak, 'If separating them is the goal, the courts would do a more certain job of it. The courts are incapable of bringing about reconciliation, but the panchayat can do that. If, today, from this place, we could send this pair of husband and wife away in reconciliation...'

'No! That can't be! I don't agree to this at all!' Bhaktiman glowered at me in anger and shouted. 'My home and my name have been ruined because of this woman. This much is certain: if I have to keep living with her, she will either murder me, or I'll have to cut my own throat. Don't you have the duty of preserving my life? I demand to be separated!'

'I too demand to be separated!' Laxmi also added.

For a moment, the panchayat was drowned in the babble of every voice talking over each other.

The sarpanch shouted to ask Bhaktiman, 'So then, do you have any wish for reconciliation at all?'

'I don't wish to reconcile.'

Laxmi was also asked, 'And you, do you wish for reconciliation, or no?'

'If he doesn't ask to be reconciled, I don't want to either.'
The panchas were perplexed.

They deliberated among themselves, asked the opinion of other people present there. Ultimately, the decision was made to grant a separation. The secretary prepared to write down the proceeds in the register.

The first question was—who would the son live with?

'My son will live with me,' Bhaktiman said. 'I can train him, give him an education. If he lives with the mother, she might elope. He will be left a destitute.'

'My son will live with me,' Laxmi said. 'He has to pay the son's expenses. I'll work to give him as much education as I can. He will bring another wife—yes, he is doing all of this just to bring home another wife. The stepmother will starve my boy, kill him through toil. Gentlemen of the panchayat—have mercy and think what the life of a motherless child is like. What does he want now, after taking away the roof over my head, after maligning my name, and now trying to snatch my son away—what it is that you want? For me to go off to live alone in a cold stone hut?'

It was decided that the son would live with Laxmi until the age of sixteen, after which he could choose whether to live with his mother or with his father.

I looked at Laxmi's face then. She was smiling with joy. I felt like smiling too, to give her company.

On the other side, Sanad was picking biscuits from his father's pocket and munching on them, swinging his legs. The father was smoothing the crumpled collar of his son's shirt.

'Now, the bits and bobs,' the sarpanch announced, making everybody laugh.

'Let her take all of her clothes,' Bhaktiman said. After a moment, he added, 'But, please, send someone from the committee. Don't let her come on her own.'

'That is appropriate,' the secretary said. 'Don't go on your own. Tell us—what do you have of your own?'

'I have eight saris.'

'How many new, and how many old?'

'Five new, three old, cotton ones.'

'She is wearing one right now,' Bhaktiman pointed out.

'There are eight more at the house.'

The secretary asked, 'What else is there?'

'Sandals, two pairs. Slippers. Two shawls. Five blouses. Two petticoats. Then there are Sanad's clothes. A ladies' coat. Umbrella, a scarf...'

'The scarf is mine, sir,' Bhaktiman said to the pancha.

'Let it be! Let her have it,' I said to Bhaktiman.

He agreed. 'All right, write it to her; the scarf too.'

'There is a suitcase, of leather...'

The secretary had already entered the suitcase into the list but Bhaktiman raised his objection, 'Not the leather suitcase, sir, but a black tin trunk. The leather suitcase isn't mine, and she knows that too.'

'Which one do you mean?' Laxmi asked Bhaktiman, as if they were bickering in their home. 'The one under Bhanubhakta's picture, near where Sanad sleeps—isn't that the family's?'

'Oh, you mean that suitcase. All right, yes, take it.' Bhaktiman laughed a little and said, 'I don't really know what is there at home.'

We all laughed upon hearing that. Our laughter helped

to lighten a bit the feeling of baseness that filled our hearts for having done the work of dividing their household.

'You have to give us mattresses and quilts too. Where will my son and I sleep otherwise?'

'What are you willing to give?' the secretary turned towards Bhaktiman to ask.

'I'll give them a blanket.'

'And a mattress?' she asked.

Bhaktiman said helplessly, 'There is but the one large mattress, of coir. If she takes that, what will I do? Lay jute sacks on the wooden bed to sleep on?'

'But there is also that dasna!'

'What dasna?' Bhaktiman asked.

'The kind they call a lampat or even a karangey; a cotton mattress, but a bit thinner,' I told him.

'If there is one, let her have it.'

'Please include a quilt,' she said to the secretary who was preparing the list.

'Then I'll keep the blanket! The blanket *and* the quilt? She'll wipe me clean! I need some things too!'

'But there are two quilts,' Laxmi said.

'Let it go! Let it be! Let her have one,' I said.

'Fine! Take it all!' Bhaktiman said. 'But even if you take everything of mine, I'll not come to you.'

'Anything else?' the secretary asked.

'I have a box, of creams and powder and brushes and combs. There was also a large mirror.'

'Aren't you ashamed to ask for the large mirror?' said Bhaktiman.

'There should be a small mirror in the cream-powder box. Make use of that for the next few days,' the secretary said.

Laxmi thought for a moment and said, 'Well—now give me dishes to cook in, and plates to eat from.'

'What do you need?'

'I have the grinding stones for spices.'

'Let her have her stone-age utensils,' I said.

'I also have a large enamel bowl.'

'If there is one that her father gave, let her have it,' Bhaktiman said. 'But I am not giving her my bowl. I need it every morning to wash my face. I'll give her a plate. Let her have a mug—that is all!'

'But you have to give her dishes in which to cook,' I said.

'Let her have two pots.'

'In what will I fill water?' she asked.

'You can buy a square tin. Why do you need a water pot?' Bhaktiman asked angrily.

'And the bowl that Sanad always eats out of?'

Bhaktiman could say nothing.

'You have to give her that,' somebody said.

'I'll keep that,' Bhaktiman said with much effort. 'Let her have another plate.'

'Is this all? Is there anything more?' the secretary asked, and read aloud the entire list.

After listening carefully, Laxmi said, 'That must be all. But please write that bowl for me. I bought it because I liked it.'

'Let her have it! Give it to her,' I said.

'What are you doing?' Bhaktiman yelled at me. 'You have given away everything I owned. If you have a bowl to give away, give it to her! That is the only one that I have. For everything, he says—"Give it away! Give it away!"'

People at the panchayat laughed out aloud.

'I'll send you a large bowl tomorrow, before you wake up. Give this one to her. Sanad will need it to bathe,' I said to him, laughing.

Bhaktiman grumbled and complained, but gave away the bowl. I looked in Laxmi's direction, expecting her to be smiling. But no—she wasn't smiling.

The panchayat was coming to an end. The only matter remaining was to fix the child and the mother's allowance.

Even in that moment, I still felt that it would be better to reconcile the two of them. With the hope that regular meetings and interactions might turn their hearts towards each other, I caught Bal Bahadur's attention and said, 'Let's fix a monthly allowance. Bhaktiman can visit his son when he goes to deliver the money. Don't you think?'

Bal Bahadur became suddenly irritated at me and said in a low growl, 'That won't do! We have to fix the amount right now, and decide everything for good.'

In the morning, while we checked together to see if the sweet peas that we had sowed a few days earlier had sprouted, Kewal's mother asked, 'What happened at the panchayat yesterday?'

I had had enough of the entire business. I said, 'What ever does happen at a panchayat? She was a blood-sucking witch. Took us some work to separate them.'

One Among Us

A buyer woke up a bunch of mustard greens sleeping on the tarmac, picked it up, matched it to himself, held it as if to make it his wife, and finally asked, 'How much for these?'

'That saag is for six paise.'

The buyer's greed gathered rage to scream injustice. He still carried the free abundance of the greens in the jungles within him. 'Wilted,' the man said, as if to suggest that he would freely reject the saag if it were wilted, and then walked away.

Maina's mother continued to wait for other customers.

'We shouldn't live in Darjeeling anymore,' a man said. 'It's full of people looking for jobs, and education won't get you anywhere anymore. We won't have enough to eat if we remain here. We were a few when we arrived, but now more people have added themselves. There isn't even enough fodder for our cattle. We must reach a new land. It doesn't rain here anymore; the trees are naked. We must go to a new land. We must ride out on horseback before the sun comes up tomorrow, with the women and children and our stuff in ox-carts. Let the strong and youthful ride before and behind the procession.

We must walk the cattle slowly. We'll travel until dusk before stopping for the night. When we have reached a distance of one hundred miles, we can decide which way to head.'

'We should take the mountain road to Assam. To the northeast.'

'Let those who come later find evidence and say: Long ago, a branch of Nepalis had built a small city named Darjeeling and settled here. Many artefacts unique to them have been unearthed. There is evidence that they busied themselves in the miniature, toy-like city for more than a century. Narrow alleys, compact machines, minuscule dwellings are found. Lacking adequate means, they had spread over the continent as nomads. Their means were insufficient, and therefore they would have perished if they had continued crowding here. The age to migrate elsewhere to expand their civilization had also passed. Therefore, in such a time of immediate need, they left home.'

'No, we have to find a new land.'

Maina's mother prepared to sprinkle water on the saag. The saag would freshen with enough water sprinkled on them, and if they could be taken to cold tap-water they would revive; she suddenly thought—everything can be kept alive here. But there was no water.

She covered the bunches of saag with a short, dirty rag. 'You've come?' she asked the woman who had come to stand by her side.

'Did the saag sell?' the woman examined the supine bunches of saag. 'How many have sold?'

'None at all.'

'Useless that I gave them here. *I* could've sold them.' The woman had carried an aeon's tiredness, and so she plopped down to the ground. 'Give me whatever money you've made. My child's father is at death's gates at home.' The woman jumped back up in panic right away.

Lines arced where each drop stepped; even from there the rain could be seen descending to the old pond. The forest resounded with the roar of rushing waters, amplifying the declarations of a torrential rain. A few bodies sprinted on a path that curved to the right around the pond. One came and stood before the tent—he was an acquaintance, he smiled. He laughed even in a rain like that and said, 'It really came down, didn't it?'

He had rolled up his trousers over his calves to sprint.

Maina's mother looked at the calves, thick as ridge-posts, and asked, just as her mother's mother had asked before her, 'Where were you going uphill?'

'I'm looking for land uphill. People have overrun the Gaushala hillside. I'm looking at a place uphill. They say Darjeeling will become a large town when it becomes full of people.'

'That is what everybody says,' he heard in reply.

Don't chat! The rain began to scream outside in admonishment. A three-stone fire-pit stood burning inside the tent; the rain trapped the smoke from the firewood inside the tent. The man with the ridge-posts calves found a low stool and sat. 'It is flooding in,' he jumped up again. The woman selling tea also stood. The rain was flooding in from the base of the tent.

'Isn't there anything to dig with?'

'No, there's nothing.'

He took a piece of firewood with him, began directing the flood away under the pelting rain. The woman saw fresh soil turned up at the base of the tent, saw that the water no longer seeped in, and saw herself ringed by a shallow channel. 'Leave it! It has stopped flooding,' she said, but the strong man continued to augment the channel.

Clouds emptied their store of rain and journeyed away. When the sun came out, the green of the forests turned yellow. The strong man was still digging up the soil.

'Will they kill this pond to build a market here?' the shop-keeper woman went to his side to ask.

'Yes, they will.'

'They'll breach the pond and drain it?'

'They'll break the pond at the farther end.'

'And it will sweep away the Gaushala village? There'll be landslides?'

'Who told you this?' he stood up to ask her.

'We are also moving uphill.'

'Are you accusing me of deserting?' he asked, finding on this day a purchase on her affections.

A man without a paisa in his pockets and clutching a small bag of rice said, 'I hear the very grass and shrubbery around here is medicinal. If we knew them, if they'd sell well, we could cut them, sell them.'

Another man who lived near her house said, 'Apparently there are mineral lodes right under our homes. Who knows— there could be a copper mine under my field. The Madhesh should be taxed on our river waters.'

A hurled stone sped past her head—*Man will reach the moon!*—and Maina's mother ducked to save herself. Another missile came to hit her on the chest—*Live as a person!*—and she crumpled over and fell. All the congregated sorrows of the world descended upon her home; all pleasures were disdainful, alien. Fearing a monstrous news that could trundle forth and run her over, she wished that she could crawl into the ground. The weight of a heavy hope sank her into the earth; she struggled to become a mountain.

'We have moved constantly to seek out places from where the mountains appear the prettiest. We don't want to move away anymore. Each of us must have a home with windows from where to watch the mountains in the morning.'

Her feverish body made her say this—'Man isn't healthy here. He is quickly satiated by anything—it's the appetite of the ailing. But a lone mountain doesn't satisfy us.'

'If we migrate to anywhere we will tie up this land in bundles and carry it away. Even the five-year-old will be made to carry his share of this inheritance.'

The bunches of saag discarded the rag and sprang to their feet. Bundles unfurled and every stem separated. They cast off their sleep and yawned. A gentle and warm evening breeze had arrived; little yellow buds of mustard swayed in it. A slender plant that had climbed high up over the branches took another radiating branch to reach even higher and suddenly became terrified with vertigo. The hand touched the grass at the base of the plant, to uproot the blades, to weed the ground. A small, slick pool of water had gathered under the tree-tomato bush—she felt like scooping it up with the rusty tin nearby to water the plant. She breathed in the joy

of having a crop growing in the terraced fields. A clump of
bamboo filled the sight. Her eyes watched a leaf fall, twirling
in its flight, having long waited for her presence. She walked
far along a parched field: the edge of the terrace was overgrown
with thick clumps of grass. She climbed up the terraces from
the far end of the fields.

> *Why did you move here?*
> *Why did you move here?*
> *Why did you move here?*
> *Why did you move here?*

A millstone in the middle of the bazaar. In the middle of the
bazaar, dining plates.

The bazaar sells knick-knacks and necessities for a thousand
homes. The millstone should watch over the entrance into
the house: it has to bind itself to the floor of the house and
become a singular body. It may not wander about; it is visited
only by the sun, either in the morning or in the evening, in
its fixed place by the entrance. Daughters and sisters of the
house discuss the matters of their hearts around it. It is never
good for it to come to the bazaar. The dark stems of chiraito
and pakhanbet should have been packed away in bundles and
in tins in every home; the plates brought to the bazaar should
have remained arranged in shelves above the stove or strewn
on the kitchen floor. Maina's mother thought of the bazaar as
a home: she felt a thousand homes had become conmingled
and strewn here. Why were a thousand homes been brought
to the bazaar to be abandoned? She had the urge to pick the
many homes and join them together. 'Sugarcanes that should
have been eaten by children, the beaten rice made by the

daughters-in-law—these should have remained at home. The stuff of our homes is kept alongside us in the bazaar. Folk left their homes first, and now their possessions have followed them to the bazaar and are waiting to persuade them to return.' Maina's mother tried to return home: she was frightened by the broad, bright afternoon of the bazaar.

> *Alerted by the din, Hanuman hid deeper in the tree*
> *Ravan hurried thither with his suit of women*
> *'When will I die by Ram's hand? I've long abducted Sita!'*
> *As he pined for Raghunath's arrival a vision favoured him.*
>
> *Sita saw the rascal approach and lowered her head.*
> *With her mind she recalled Shri Ram's feet to her heart.*

She looked around to keep herself alert. Dark blobs of men climbed stairs, chatted. Their gossip didn't pause, the eyes roved here and there and saw other people. Sight had become sound, those visible spoke, separated, those being looked at became hidden. Bags and tarps waved and collided.

A shadow the colour of a flag passed, a mike's blaring halted at the ears. A little boy ran. Three people came and went—one lost in thoughts, others rushing with purpose. 'I was born here, I'll stay here. This is what I have and this is what I'll sell. I must find happiness in the things I possess—here is my foothold.' A dog chased, ran past, reached far. 'Rags and papers!' voices shouted. The bazaar continued to convulse, continued to scratch its itch and show impatience.

The sun had been placed atop an electricity pole. 'Why did you come here?' Somebody, unseen and close, asked her. 'Why did you come?' The wandering voice of the bazaar asked.

A man walking ahead of her turned around to ask her the same question. People on the streets came, one queue after another, to ask her the same. People inside buildings opened their windows to ask the same question—high voices, sharp voices, and wide-open mouths all directed their questions at her. She covered her face with a dirty shawl and from its small window peered outside with her ancient fear. The entire bazaar abandoned its duties to rush to her, surround her with a thousand faces and ask: 'Why did you come here?'

'They'll trample over my mustard greens,' her fear became acute. She threw herself over the bunches of saag.

At dusk, she was eagerly selling saag. When night draped overhead she placed a wooden box and an upturned basket to claim her spot for the next day.

Long Night of Storm

The storm had begun rattling the tin kerosene-can sheets nailed to the roof with a monotonous *khaltaang-khaltaang khat-khat*. It filled the heart with the dread that it would blow the roof away.

In the dim flicker of the lamp stirred by the wind, Kaley's parents glanced up at the roof-ridge. Fine beads of moisture— like the sheen of sweat—appeared on a few of the tin-sheets blackened by firewood soot. Equally sooty rafters of cherry and poplar wood anchored the eighty or ninety tin-sheets against the wind.

'How the wind howls over this hill!' Kaley's mother said after the storm let up some, and began lighting a fire in the hearth.

'Doesn't halt at all,' Kaley's father added. 'Today makes it a whole week!'

He had barely spoken the words when the rain started pouring in a torrent—*dha-ra-ra-ra…*

'And, when it rains, there's the worry about landslides,' Kaley's father said. 'We were fools to settle on this spot.'

It started raining even more fiercely. Tongues of flame in

the hearth leapt and danced with the deafening din from the tin-sheets on the roof. As the storm raged harder, the individual tattoo of raindrops melded to become an uninterrupted roar that radiated in all directions. *Soon, everything will be swept away, pulled away by a landslide, a deluge of soil that blankets from above...*

They felt: a landslide is sweeping away this home; it is pulling us with it.

'Mahakal Baba! You are our protector and keeper!'

Rain swept sideways by the storm hit the wall planks. The planks were all wet on the inside too.

The bed that was usually set against the wall had been shifted to a spot where the water didn't drip. Kaley was asleep, with his sister in his arms.

'We built the house on a spot like this because of your stubbornness,' the husband suddenly said angrily. 'We were comfortable living in a building in the bazaar, and with my job as a policeman. Without the fear of storms or the worry of landslides...'

The wife said nothing.

'Work the land now! See where your greed has got you!'

'Go and sleep, quit worrying,' she finally said. 'This is how the rains are in July. Can't be helped—it is the same every year. If a landslide kills us, then we die! What can be done if death comes for us?'

'You came seeking death. And you'll find it too.'

By and by, the downpour abated. The wife made her husband a mug of tea.

When the rain let up significantly, even the water falling off the eaves became audible.

He sipped his tea and asked, 'What time do you think it is now?'

'Who knows what hour! May be eleven, twelve o'clock...' she said, and yawned twice.

'Will it stop now?'

'It should.'

He stood up after finishing his tea. He must have kicked a pot set to catch rain-drip, because it spilled. 'Watch your steps,' the wife said, and brought out a jute sack to spread.

He said nothing.

When he opened the door to the darkness outside and listened, the river Rung Dung roared fearsomely, setting the hillsides juddering. When he thought he heard other noises intermingled with the river's roar, he imagined the river sweeping with it an entire trunk of a drooping fig, or of the river coloured ochre with the mud from a landslide. The darkness was thick enough to hide his arms.

He returned and, without entering the house, called to his wife from the darkness outside, 'The torch! Bring me the torch!'

She found the old black torchlight from under the pillow and took it to him.

'The tin sheets over the cattle-shed have been blown away,' he said, lit the torchlight, and climbed below the hut. An eye-shaped torch-beam appeared on the wet ground and damp grass.

Kaley's mother also followed at his heels.

As they entered the cattle-shed, the cow, which had been slumped on the ground, stood abruptly and let out a bellow. Rain dripping from the roof had wet the cow's back, and its hair was stuck together.

Kaley's father climbed to the roof of the cattle-shed after collecting pieces of the wind-strewn tarp. He arranged the tin sheets and weighed them down with rocks.

It was still drizzling.

Kaley's mother searched for and found a large, round rock, slick with algae, and passed it to her husband on the roof. After setting it on the roof her husband said, 'Go now. It's started pouring again. I'll give them fodder and come.'

'Let's go together,' the wife said. She waited.

'Then you go ahead and give them fodder. I'll arrange this, and… But who will show me the torch-light? Wait! Wait—I'm almost done…'

And, as she waited, the rain drenched through her shawl and washed over her face. Her husband finally finished and climbed down. They hurriedly set out the fodder and went into the house.

Once more, the rain came pouring down.

By the time they had finished changing out of their clothes they looked ready to act the part of beggars in a drama. They started a roaring fire and began warming and drying by it.

'Is there tea?' he asked.

'Shouldn't we go to bed?' a question arrived in lieu of an answer.

'You sleep. Put on some tea for me.'

Kaley's mother pulled a blackened kettle and used a mug to draw water into it.

'Fill it to the brim,' he said.

His wife did just that.

He was staring at the roof. He stood up, found the twine he had stashed away under the rafters to braid into a rope, and began tying down the roof. He was searching for a place to anchor the free end when he saw the millstone.

'Bring that to me!'

'Why?'

'The wind is the devil!'

Kaley's mother couldn't refuse. She rolled the millstone to his feet.

He felt somewhat relaxed after tying the braid of the rope to the millstone.

After throwing a sprinkling of tea-leaves into the kettle, Kaley's mother climbed into bed.

Her husband was left alone, pondering. Only when the tea boiled over and its foaming water fell into the fire did he startle from this thoughts.

He was making tea when the wind picked up again and something fell on the roof with a bang. A branch of alder? He was utterly terrified.

When the rain and the wind ceased and it became tranquil he climbed into bed without blowing out the lamp.

The radish seeds sowed in the afternoon must have been swept away, he thought. Dykes along the terraces must have crumbled and crushed so many marigold plants. The next day, the first thing in the morning, a channel would need to be cut above the house, away from the wormwood bush.

Had he slept at all? When he awoke, the storm and rain roared at a fiendish pitch. As if to blow the house away— picking it in jolts. The wind was howling through and the rain thrashing on the trees around with a frightening roar.

He woke his wife.

'It is blowing hard outside, Maili! What should we do?'

She had hardly been able to respond when the entire floor of the house shuddered and juddered…

'Get up! Something's wrong!'

He grabbed the torch and went to open the door. His wife came and stood behind him. When he shone the torch and looked carefully he saw that an edge of the yard had crumbled and slipped. A mulberry tree slowly tipped over and fell with the landslide.

'What are we going to do now?' she cried out of fear.

'Go! Wake the kids,' he commanded his wife, shouting over the din of the rain. When his wife left, he turned off the torchlight and stood at the threshold, watching.

And, gradually, through the rain and the fog, he imagined he saw the faint light of a new dawn approach. A mature rooster kept under a bamboo basket inside the house crowed to dispel any doubt—*Kukhuree-kaan! Kukhuree-ee-ee-ee-kaan!*

In the morning, as Kaley's mother walked to the bazaar with a bamboo tub of milk, her husband, who was routing the floodwater with a spade, yelled to remind her, 'Nails! Long nails—don't forget! We have to nail everything down through the day!'

'If it keeps raining hard, don't send Kaley to school,' she said and climbed the hill. A side of the hill on the way had fallen across the road. She didn't see any of the folks she usually met on the way.

After about an hour and a half, she arrived at Moktan's, near the court. They usually took half a litre of milk. While she was measuring out the milk, the young, pretty wife showed kindness and said, 'Come and sit inside. Drink a warm cup of tea before you leave.' Kaley's mother shut her umbrella, stood it by the door, and went inside.

'What a storm it was last night!' she said. 'We haven't slept a wink.'

'We haven't either,' the young wife said. 'The storm banged this window all night—*ghitik-ghitik, ghitik-ghitik*. I just couldn't sleep. What a nasty storm it was!'

'Was that all?' Kaley's mother, dark of face and full-bodied, approaching forty years of age, said dismissively. 'The wind nearly blew away our house. What do you have to worry about here? You don't have the fear of landslides here. It swept away all of our yard. Now it is about to take the house. The rain is no excuse for us—we can't leave the cow hungry; we have to run about to find it fodder. We can't sleep through the day just because we couldn't sleep in the night...'

'We are safe only in name,' the young wife said with sympathy. 'The roof leaked and drenched all the clothes, all the books. And the power goes out just then...'

'No, no; compared to us, you have no fear. See, if it begins raining, my mind begins to worry what might have happened at home while I am away. The wind knocked down all of our maize crop, it left nothing standing...'

Kaley's mother left to deliver milk elsewhere.

'We brought this misery upon ourselves out of a greed to work the fields,' she increasingly felt in her heart. 'Otherwise, we were living comfortably in the bazaar. There was a salary at the end of each month, and it had somehow been enough. The children had their school close by, it was no trouble to fetch water, the roads were good and convenient. There was no fear either of storms or of landslides. We invited this trouble upon ourselves for nothing by greeding after land.

'I haven't had a moment's rest since we bought the land. Fingers sliced by sickles, palms cracked by dung and dust— it is embarrassing to show ourselves before others. I can't leave home even for a day—any wish to visit farther afield is impossible. I'll have to grind away just like this until I die.

'And this slow grind to death—is it for this meagre living, to be so poorly fed and clothed? And, what really have we to eat and wear? We have to hide our food out of shame of being seen, and we are ashamed to stand alongside others in these rags.'

In her heart raged a gale of many angry thoughts.

Soon she reached the house of the constable to deliver milk.

After she knocked on the glass pane of the closed door and announced, 'Milk!', a young girl in a dirty frock came to receive the milk. As she was pouring out the usual litre and half of milk, the constable's wife shouted from inside, 'Grandma! Please bring an extra three litres tomorrow to make rice-pudding!'

After wavering for a moment for some reason, she told the young girl to carry her message. 'Tell her there won't be enough to spare. It is getting impossible to give everybody their share. Then there is the storm... I don't even know if I'll come tomorrow. Tell her to find it elsewhere...'

The constable's wife must have heard her, because now she came to the door, looked at the wet clothes on Kaley's mother, and said, 'Please, do bring it! Where else will I go looking for milk in rain like this? Please bring it! Only because it is Deepak's birthday...'

'Won't be enough!' A tired and bitter utterance emerged from her core. She watched the constable's wife—how clean were her clothes, how fair the face, how pretty the hands! Her husband lives in comfort. There are beds and couches all over the house, and wardrobes full of sarees. Doesn't need to touch soil or mud, doesn't have to fear gale or rain.

'Won't be enough. And, if it keeps raining like this, I won't come tomorrow.'

'Do you want us to drink black tea all day long? What are you even saying! Please bring it. No matter what—just bring it!'

Kaley's mother said nothing, climbed down the steps and headed towards the bazaar.

And, as she walked alone, she muttered to herself, 'No! This mad insistence to live in constant fear of landslides and storms and toil over two acres of land, two crops a year, to make a living, is to push the family towards murder. I'll sell the heifers and the two milk cows all together for a lumpsum. Even if it is in a small room rented for five or six rupees, I'll live in the bazaar itself. I could sell greens and vegetables at the chowk—just like Thuli's mother does. Husband knows carpentry, and he knows masonry. If not that, he'll find work as a watchman. I'll bring up my two children in ease. I'm not going to live amid such desolation anymore…'

She felt reassured after being able to make the decision. The aches in her feet disappeared. She didn't care that the rain wet her.

And, buoyed by a sudden joy, she went towards the snacks shop on the main street. She bought roasted peas and grams worth two annas and put it in her bag. She asked a tailor woman who had come to the shop to buy green peas, 'Is there an empty room around where you live?'

'No. Why? Was there a landslide where you live?'

'No, I am looking for a place around the bazaar. Somewhere close to water taps. Between ten and fifteen rupees to rent.'

'There is one room,' the gaunt tailor woman said. 'A Madhesi was paying twelve, excluding the two rupees for electricity. He has left. I can let you know tomorrow.'

'I'll come to your place. I'll come around this time.'

She walked towards Maalgodam, safe under her umbrella. She needed to deliver milk to two more places before returning.

When she reached B. B. Gurung's verandah, she saw that a crowd had gathered there since early in the morning—a few of them even stood outside, under open umbrellas, talking. She walked around the back to deliver milk. She couldn't tell what had happened. Something must have befallen either the husband or the wife; they were childless. The fat wife walked in and out of the house all day, smacking her slippers on the floor, sometimes reaching farther into the bazaar, cradling her white cat, Nini. The husband had a dry-cleaning business on Ladenla road.

'What happened? Why is there a crowd here?' she asked the woman from next door who came to collect the milk instead.

'Nini's mother fell in the night. She's unconscious. Still hasn't come around.'

'Where did she fall?'

She heard the story:

The cat was locked out during the big storm of the night. It must have meowed so much, but the rain didn't let it be heard. When the rain abated a bit, they searched for the cat. They searched outside, they called out to the cat, but it didn't come. When she went down the steps to search, Nini's mother's shoes slipped, and she fell down on the road. They rushed to fetch the doctor, but the doctor didn't arrive soon enough. She still hadn't regained consciousness.

'And all for a lousy cat!' Kaley's mother muttered softly. 'Isn't this the cat?'

The white cat sat in the warmth of the stove, licking its fur.

She couldn't abruptly rise and walk away. She continued to sit on the doorsill.

As she sat there, she saw the husband come out of the house crying. She heard—the woman had died.

'How absurd!' she muttered to herself, and slung across her shoulders her bag with the container of milk.

After reaching the watchman's house, measuring out a quarter litre, and after pouring out a splash for the baby girl who brought a cup, Kaley's mother slumped on the empty sack laid out on the floor.

The watchman's wife took off the boiling tea from the stove, put the milk on, and asked, 'How is it around your place? The storm must have wreaked havoc, must have ruined everything...'

Kaley's mother was lost in thoughts; she didn't respond.

The watchman's wife said again, 'There is no danger here in the bazaar, no fear. But in the tea gardens and bustees, I know how difficult it is, what sort of destitution. That is why our fathers settled in the bazaar.'

Now, recalling some strength, Kaley's mother said, 'Peril and calamity are everywhere. Yes, the storm ruined things, but we will fix everything now—it is nothing impossible to do. We have our own home, a cattle-shed full of cows. A field, and in the field some thirty or forty groves of bamboo, gooseberry and fig trees, and cucumber vines reaching the skies. How much more ruin can a storm bring? See, I have to rush now, get home and rebuild.'

And, after hurriedly sipping the tongue-scalding hot tea, she reached the bazaar to buy the nails.

And, to herself, she muttered, 'It is already very late. Kaley's father is going to kill me today!'

The Ordinariness of a Day

'You've sown the radish seeds very sparsely,' I said. I was loosening the tamped down earth with a piece of dry bamboo. 'But the shower from the other day has sprouted them all.'

I had trampled down a clump of long grass growing on the edge of the terrace to sit on. She sat on a bag from which I had finished sowing bean seeds. We were resting. The long terraces immediately below us were full of new radishes—they already showed new leaves in pairs and threes through the recently hoed soil.

'The rain swept away some seeds, but our hen also doesn't let any seed sprout,' Maya said. 'The mother of nine chicks always climbs down here.'

'Yes, she does...'

'If I don't watch her even for a second, she digs up the entire hillside.'

'Isn't it hot today? The sort that ripens the corn?'

'We'll recoup the cost of the seeds,' Maya was still talking about the radishes.

'What did I just say?' I pretended to be angry.

'What else? You said it was sunny today, that the corn will ripen.' Maya laughed feebly.

'Let the sun shine like this for another week,' I said. 'All our corn will ripen, the cucumbers will grow bigger, the tree-tomatoes hanging from their branches will get colour.'

'Both of my brooding hens will hatch their chicks, I'll have finished getting the potatoes dug up, and the beans you have planted today will have sprouted,' she added.

'Dashain will be just a month and a half away, we should finish buying new dresses for the children by then, I'll have received my salary, and bought your honour your Kanjeevaram sari.'

Maya laughed. 'See—they've finished planting,' she pointed.

At the top of his fields some distance from us, Sanbir's father rested to roll tobacco in a leaf. He must have finished planting the saplings.

'Everybody should have a small jungle of his own. Not because he can gather fodder from there for his cow and the firewood for his stove. But because the neighbours are bound to ask, and so he can be giving. And they're bound to steal, and so he can pretend to shout at them. That's worldliness. Thick ears of maize will grow there; let our children see them and be awed. Ainselu berries will smother their thorny branches; let the neighbours swarm for a taste.'

'It's been two days since the sun has come out like this,' Maya said.

And, indeed, the sun was out in all of its glory; it brought warmth all around, making the air muggier with each climb down to the next terrace. The breeze was hugging the stream in its uphill climb, shaking cardamom, tiger grass and maney leaves. On this side, the tall stalks of maize screening us from the breeze each carried a pair of maize ears.

'We have a good harvest of maize this year,' I said. 'Even rats and crows will come to feed on it.'

My eyes reached all the way to the lowest terrace.

'The householder's is the most superior of all the dharmas, our grandmother used to tell us. Even sadhus and sages have to beg to eat, but the householder feeds everyone, from man to the gods, from the birds to the mice.'

This bit about dharma must have engrossed me.

'Perhaps,' I said. 'But to live such a dharma of the householder, things have to be saved from thieves. We have to pelt stones at those who steal.'

'Poor Sainla-daju guards his maize field all day long. He watches over it even on Sundays,' Maya said. 'If the monkeys get half a second they pillage the entire harvest.' She tried to look up at Sainla Newar's cornfield, but the walls of our fields blocked her sight.

'His fields are at the edge of the forest. They'll enter our fields only after finishing with his.' I had nothing to worry about.

'Sanbir's father really must have finished planting saplings. Our children have gone there, too.' She had spotted them. I, too, saw flashes of green and white.

'And the boy went there without a shirt on his back!'

'We planted trees, but you brought too many champak saplings,' Maya said.

'There are champaks that don't flower. They make good fodder,' I said. 'We should be planting lots of tussare cuttings around this season. They do grow, don't they?'

'What is the point in growing tussare? It isn't a winter fodder—it sheds leaves before that. It is green in monsoon, but there is plenty of green grass around then. For fodder, gogun is the best.'

'Gogun is best.'

'Gogun also adorns the field.'

A gogun tree nodded above us, eavesdropping. Its thick canopy blocked out the blue of the sky above.

'Tell me, what in particular is beautiful about the gogun?' I asked, examining the tree.

'The foliage is impressively dense—isn't that what makes it beautiful?' I also answered my own question.

'The red rib that grows from the base to the tip of the leaf, see—on every leaf—that's what I like about it.'

Many a moment passed.

'Look over there,' I pointed towards the slopes of Sikkim. 'Denzong is just over that peak. Look! Clouds! How they swirl there! How pretty!'

Maya rested her frailty against me and looked in that direction.

'Tell me, how would I phrase it if I wrote it into a story?'

'How would I know?'

'The mountain gathers a brood of clouds in its lap... No, that doesn't work, does it?'

'No, it doesn't.' Maya laughed.

'The clouds seek to seep into the rocks and hide forever,' I said out of stubbornness.

'Like the Dali painting?' she asked. 'We saw it the other day?'

I forfeited the enterprise.

We watched other families' lands farther afield. Terraces cut like waves of water, terraces of grass and earth.

'How many clumps of bamboo do we have?' I asked suddenly.

'Twenty.'

'There are twenty-eight clumps of pareng alone. Twenty-nine with the one I brought last year—the one with the small, fluttery leaves.'

'Did it take root?'

'Why wouldn't it?'

'I had really liked the bamboo in Phulbari, with the square stems, one culm green and another yellow. I liked that.'

'The one by the pond?'

Maya laughed.

'I'll bring that for you.'

'I had showed it to you last year,' Maya spoke with disappointment, but with hope in her heart.

'No good comes out of planting fig. Any big storm snaps the branches off, breaks the trunk itself. Only the two plants in the hollow have done well.'

'Renuka's mother isn't any more since yesterday either,' I continued. 'The children cry with such heartrending wails when it is time to take away the body. I am terrified of that moment's crying.'

I paused, lost in thought.

'Of course the children will cry,' Maya said.

'The children cry fiercely on that day, while the husband silently endures it all. But the children begin to forget as the days pass, and with every passing day they begin to laugh a little more, and in a while they entirely forget to cry because their whole life stands before them in wait, carrying with it bundles of hopes and desires. But the husband who didn't cry on the day remembers his wife when somebody else gives him his food in the evening, he remembers her when he prepares to go to bed, and when he wakes in the morning he remembers again that she is gone, and he remembers her while he is busy at work outside and he remembers her when he enters their home and sits down to rest. He continues to be startled by this realization as long as he lives.'

'Now he lives only out of the compulsion of life itself.' This, too, I added.

The sun was splashed over the tea estates across the valley, a sunlight where all shades of green were lit bright.

Narrow roads, ruts of walking paths descended from a mess of houses; a line zigged and zagged and encircled a clump of eight or ten trees before entering it—the village's water spring must have been there. Another path climbed upward from the village into the forest, to gather firewood; torrents of white monsoon descended, slicing through the estate in three places. Foamy stitches of a creek also rushed down the hill, and the bigger river below shook the base of the mountains. There was a place in the forest where a waterfall fell into another waterfall; I searched for it after the rains every year.

'If you keep searching, you can see water falling from there.' She also pointed to the same place.

And, if you waited, as if in a stupor, water did slush forth to fall slowly. Joy swept up.

I went close and said, 'We have a good harvest of soybeans in the fields this year. Our maize is the best. We don't have any marigold but our potatoes have revived.'

'You're a white-collar man, and I am ill,' Maya said. I looked at her face, blushing on this day with a sheen of sweat. She had tired of contemplating the graveness of life, and now she teased me. 'Trying to cut a bunch of these knotwoods or a handful of wood sorrel could bring upon a fever... Or the rain could catch me by the door for half a minute and I could die.'

'"Chamey's wife Gaunthali had a sharp tongue. Even when one spoke to her sincerely she found reasons to quarrel,"' I recited.

Maya laughed. My accusation was excessive, and she laughed because she couldn't parry the bit that was beyond the reasonable. That was her weakness. I pitied her.

As we watched, a hole-riddled, expansive net of fog swirled straight up and spread out above us.

'Don't sit in the cold too long. Let's go,' I said.

'I feel hot,' she said.

I stood first, then she took my arm to stand up.

'Look, your acidanthera there has flowered too.' On the edge of a lower terrace danced two pairs of white blossoms rising from slender green stems; the breeze carried a sharp streak of its fragrance.

'I have planted pretty cypress trees.' I surveyed the field. 'The pear tree over there has grown tall. The wild pear will start giving fruit next year. That tree is of large mulberries— don't let anybody cut it down.'

We were walking back along the edge of the terraces. We started by brushing aside the drooping leaves of the broom grass and losing our way among the maize grown taller than us.

'Wait, I'll pick some ears of maize,' Maya stopped to search for ripe ears. I reached above her and broke off a couple.

When we had climbed a bit I said, 'Receive your blessings. If you want to keep me pleased, always make me a chutney of this.' An enticing bush of timur peppercorns flourished with tiny red thorns all over its stems and leaves.

'Oh, your fancies…'

'What is for the curry today?' I asked.

'Cauliflower. I'll send Deshpad later to pick one.'

'Aren't we eating chicken?'

'Which one?'

'That one-eyed spotted rooster.'

'Kill it.'

She was walking ahead of me, carrying the maize in her shawl. I turned her around and said, 'We are a grand prince and his princess. We had come to see how our subjects fared, to gauge and experience their joys and sorrows. We have spent twelve long years in disguise and assessed everything. We can no longer endure this life. Let us return to our royal palace.'

Maya laughed, softly.

'I was going to say something,' she said, 'but I won't. Let it be.'

When we reached the yard, Madhu, Alpana and other children had returned, had drawn hop-scotch tiles and were playing. I stole our youngest daughter's turn and hopped through the boxes.

'Am I right?'

I shut my eyes. It was quiet, and I waited for somebody to answer.

Kheer

I hadn't understood the incident at the time, and I had failed to imagine that perhaps it contained a meaning. The incident—let's call it an incident—had transpired thus:

Although I had encountered repeatedly in short stories and novels—and, later, written in my own works—descriptions of the Teesta's muted roar, I'd never really had the opportunity to listen to the song of the Teesta to my heart's content. I had heard from folks who toiled along its banks in the months of monsoon and winter about how the Teesta sighed long smothering sighs at noon and at midnight. However, the hurried stops on the bridge to look upriver and downriver and briefly listen to the Teesta during my rushed travels to Kalimpong and Gangtok had left my hunger and thirst for the Teesta's song unsated. Traces of innumerable pasts drawn on the slumbering sands above the blue-green expanse of water that brought to mind the word 'immense'; reeds and the jungles along the banks swaying, fanned by a breeze, and, within that imagined picture, I would recollect, folded within the roar of Teesta's song, a separate lapping of waves and distinct gurgles and murmurs...

It was for this reason that I had made up my mind

to spend the night by the Teesta on my way home from Gangtok.

Perhaps because the rooms in the Dak Bungalow were being repaired, the room given to me had also been recently given a wash of lime and therefore was disconcertingly bright and white, the odour of the whitewash pervasive. The workers engaged in repairing the Dak Bungalow—the carpenters and plasterers, painters and coolies—were staying in the adjacent room, and they make up the plot of this story. They were making it a day of celebrations, and so they were congregated in the room, eagerly talking over each other. Some were cooking, and that was at the heart of their conversation: they were cooking kheer.

I detest conversations about food. But left without a choice, I continued listening to them. Outdoors was the stunned brightness of an afternoon. By the time I looked out after spreading the bedding on the cot, a different hue of light—as if suddenly a lot more of the evening had intruded—poured through the innermost leaves and branches of trees.

'If you really want kheer, you need two litres of milk for every quarter kilo of rice,' said an assertive voice that suggested a face with deep-set eyes. 'For our rice we need about ten litres. How much did you use?'

'How much would it be? Just the four litres…'

'And you're making a four-litre-milk kheer in a place like Teesta? Shame!' the voice from earlier said. 'Kheer made with four litres of milk!' he added, as if the point he was making was a black rag riddled with holes which he was showing everyone.

'If you really want to make kheer you need many more

ingredients,' an older voice boomed. 'You don't have the right kind of rice to begin with. You need the nooniya strain, fine and smooth…'

'Even the aluwa rice is unaffordable here,' said a voice that perhaps belonged to a reserved man. 'And then they pass off local hill rice as Rangoon aluwa.'

'That trash looks just like the bayerni rice from the hills,' another chimed in helpfully.

'I meant, if we really had everything we needed and really wanted to have kheer,' the older voice marched on, 'Nooniya rice, aged, even better if it is the black nooniya—it is fragrant—cook it in ten or twelve litres of undiluted milk. You'll need fifteen litres if you use the diluted sort. By the time the five extra litres of water evaporate, the rice breaks up and becomes a paste—mush. But if your milk is thick as a fist the rice grains keep their shape, it becomes the best kind of kheer. The mushy kind sticks to the pot and burns, it will smell burnt to whoever eats last…'

'Taste like cleaning teeth with charcoal,' perhaps somebody else said something similar, but I didn't hear him clearly.

In a while, another voice boiled over from another corner, 'As if it is enough to have just the milk! You need pistachios, raisins, walnuts, cinnamon, coconut, bay leaves, cloves. Cook it at just the right, low heat. Add the raisins at the very end. Too early, and they burst open.'

'What happens if you add all of that?' an enthusiastic, young voice asked.

'Flavour!' 'For fragrance!' 'Gives you power!' All other voices clamoured at him.

'Don't get used to it,' a voice continued, as if to deliver

the dregs of a collective contempt, 'or you'll wander in your dreams, searching for kheer. That'll be the only comfort you'll get.'

'If you cook kheer here in that way, its aroma will hit somebody walking on the road way over there,' another added.

And, just then, I put some effort into trying to smell their kheer, but I couldn't manage the faintest whiff of it.

'Your kheer! We can't smell it sitting right here,' the old man also added.

'When I said let's not scrimp on anything, let's eat some great kheer, you refused money,' came a response in protest. 'Be it by earning it, or through theft, or with leaving debts unpaid, a man should eat well, a man must be able to eat well and live.'

Everybody went silent.

I found that I too was attending to that sudden silence. I rose defiantly and began pacing about in the room. This declaration of my presence acted as a catalyst, as if a large boulder had fallen into the stream of their conversation and forced it into a new direction.

'It's not enough just to get everything together—you have to have the skills to cook,' a man started, his voice tepid as pale steam.

'There's no point in eating kheer willy-nilly, whenever you feel like. It has to be at the right time, under the right conditions,' another added.

'It is hard, then, to eat kheer,' a third voice lamented bitterly. 'Impossible!'

I looked out, barely able to suppress my laughter. All seemed ordinary. The dark trees of dusk stood at attention.

'Keep stirring, or even this piddling bit of kheer will burn.'

'It must be ready now.'

'It's done! Yes!'

'Cooked enough, yes.'

With grunts of 'Yes, it's cooked, definitely', etc., the pot was taken off the fire. I imagined men shifting away, perhaps a few picking and occupying favoured spots.

As they ate, someone asked, 'Something smells, doesn't it?'

'It does.'

'It is the firewood. I've been noticing it for some time now,' someone else said.

In cycles, doubt died, resurrected.

'It isn't sweet enough,' somebody said, walked a few paces to fetch the sugar and sprinkle it over his share.

'If you really want decent kheer,' the same voice which had cooked up the conversation initially spoke through mouthfuls, 'it isn't sugar you should use, but molasses. Gives it colour.'

'And not molasses of sugarcane, but the layered, clean molasses of the toddy-palm—only then is the kheer genuinely luscious,' a second voice supplied immediate editorial correction. 'Who would eat kheer with sugarcane molasses! Disgusting!'

'What is this talk about eating? You get some kheer after so many days and you can't stop talking about it. I am embarrassed for you.' The man who said this must have aimed to have me hear him and lighten his own shame.

And soon, they busied themselves with eating.

'Nothing but sweetened rice and milk,' when the man with the deep voice spoke, everybody burst into laughter. The skilled cook continued to laugh for the longest. And, as he stopped and started abruptly to chortle, his comrades also joined in the laughter.

I understand the significance of that incident now, four years after that evening. The kheer that they cooked is representative of life: our hearts are full of ideals dictating to us that life ought to be lived in a certain manner, that life should be put to work in our service in specific ways, or that a particular sort of utility must be wringed from it, but the errors, absences, insufficiencies and ruinations in the lives that we live in reality colour our experience of life to resemble their kheer, which was but merely a satire aimed at the ideal of kheer.

Can life ever be like the Teesta which, without prejudice to where or how it flows, always remains an ideal?

Journey of an Ideal

To send the daughter to school every day—she asks me to adjust her belt, she goes to school, and all of this is life, and life is merely this. Perhaps I will never accomplish great deeds, but I am capable of tightening the belt on my daughter's frock; and that of which I am capable is the whole of life. The tasks that can be accomplished within this day's length—there is no need to look to the future—potato and maize seeds necessary for the coming year's sowing: only these are life and its ingredients. Man has adulterated life with a surfeit of elements and made it into poison.

I was attempting to identify the direction from which this desperate, angst-ridden thought had jogged casually into my mind.

Mysteries fall into our lives and fill it with a sweet ache; such mysteries that confront our existence in the sudden paleness of an evening, or in the wakefulness of the hours past midnight when in the rain-hours it begins to drizzle. Without these, life would be no more than a blank brightness. I, too, have purchased mysteries. The tattoo of rain on the roof, the nightlong drip-drip of rainwater from the eaves to the ground are dear to me. And, somehow, when the feriwal comes around in the night to blow his horn, I wake up; the feriwal blows his horn again, without strain, and walks around the house, chanting in a deep voice words that I don't comprehend. The dog in the house also remains quiet; to my ears, the feriwal's heavy steps make it seem that he has walked far away. I am still straining to hear his calls.

I believe that I had become frightened and run to my father when I heard a feriwal for the first time as a child. Babu had woken up. I must have asked him all sorts of questions, because Babu said, 'You'll see him tomorrow.'

The feriwal had come to the door in the morning. Aama brought out a nanglo. I spied from a hole in the wall. Whether it was Aama's shawl or the feriwal's clothes, I saw a flash of white.

'Why did you give the feriwal so many things on the nanglo? Turmeric, salt, rice, lentils?' I asked.

'He'll fight and chase away evil spirits,' Aama said.

Spirits of the dark roamed in the night, perhaps watched us in our sleep. Through eyes torn wide I could see their shapes, darker than the dark, standing and stealing forward.

'The feriwal goes out alone in such hours.'

In your hearts dark mysteries begin to gather.

Another feriwal visited on another night some time later. A cascade of moonlight had fallen from the skies to spray itself inside the house. I got out of bed and stealthily parted the curtains to peep outside.

It was a man shrouded in a large white shawl. He went

downhill past our house. The dog snarled a little well after he had passed, pretended to bark once.

When I had grown up sufficiently, I became capable of looking my idols directly in the eye. Therefore, one morning, after offering him many things, I asked, 'I can't understand a word of what you chant. What do feriwals like you really say, brother?'

He said that they were devotees of Shiva. He asked me to note down a line: *Where the jogi blows his feri horn, there is the lord's protection.*

I thought of Shiva, of his age. Certainly, Shiva was a person, from a mountain somewhere under the Himalaya, of a certain place and of a certain time. His shelter was security to sufferers. It was the age of valour. He would blow his horn into the four directions; the reach of his horn's blast was his realm, his right and his peace. The rival who heard the horn and remained quiet accepted defeat.

'Even today my feriwals blow their horns in the night to challenge all rival powers.'

One day, I had reached Simana, the border town. The day was overcast; after loading firewood onto a truck we accompanied the contractor to his home which was also a tea-shop.

We entered the house through the shop. It was a soot-darkened, dim chamber. My feet stepped on a man.

When we step on a person, we know it even through the soles of our shoes. I stopped, froze. The man didn't say anything, didn't move. It felt unnatural, inadequate. 'What's here?' I asked.

The householder, who had already walked ahead, replied, 'There's a feriwal jogi sleeping.'

'What?' I gasped.

I set foot with care. It was as if my foot had fallen off. I stepped on yet another man.

'How many are there?' I shouted angrily.

The householder had already passed through to light. He answered with irritation, 'There must be twenty-five or thirty.'

'Twenty-five? Thirty?' I seem to have asked, peered into the darkness of the soot-smeared room and gasped, 'Thirty feriwals!'

Thirty feriwals in the same place! I found the number and the gathering abhorrible. That there could be a congregation of feriwals, that they could be many and plural, that one of them could be the same as another of them had never entered my imagination. My feriwal was a solitary creature, walking alone, never knowing of any other feriwal. I have always seen statues of the Nepali tiger as solitary creatures; a tiger is formidable as it is—supplied with wings, it may come soaring over oceans; but I am revolted by the idea of an army of such tigers. There can only ever be one such tiger in this world.

I came to their room. I saw that they had opened one of the higher windows and light had entered the room. Two of them had woken up and had dug up embers from the ashes in the hearth; the fire no longer smoked. On the earthen floor stretched many straight and bent bodies, each pulling a dirty shawl to cover his face. A whiff of the mingled odours of little men and their dirty and dusty clothes. A kind of oppression reigned in the room.

After arriving at the bazaar at Suke, I reported everything to an older acquaintance. He said, 'That is how every ideal topples, one by one. There is but one eternal ideal: God.'

But God as an ideal had fallen a long time ago for me.

An ideal, of a mystery of mine, had lapsed today, and another will fall tomorrow—of patriotism, of virtue, of literariness—and gradually all my ideals will become depleted. And, after that, am I to continue wearing this life as if a tattered rag?

Swindlers and beggars of all mintage come to stand before the door of the house. Therefore, my house has a rule: to the disabled and the helpless we happily give coins, a handful of grains, tea, an old coat. If a swindler comes and stands at the door, in accordance with the household rule, we give him a squash fruit. There are always squash fruits strewn all over the gully in the backyard, so we give them one. The swindlers accept even that, demonstrate their humility and helplessness, and leave.

They said the horn was blown again last night; a feriwal was standing at the door with his multi-coloured bag. The wife had prepared a large platter of foodstuff to offer, but I stopped her, picked up a squash fruit and gave him that.

The feriwal looked at me with scorn, refused my offering, walked away.

One of my ideals had certainly been shattered, but the person and psyche that I am hadn't been chipped in the least—I was alive and whole even if a little worn. I found joy and strength at the door: forget just the one ideal, even when the entire store of a man's ideals are destroyed, his psyche remains whole.

I have become much stronger after bearing this blow and I can say this emphatically: Man didn't have ideals earlier, but his 'life' was truthful and whole. To deny this is to blaspheme against life. The exercise of collecting ideals came much later, and more and more ideals were added. But life can be lived without adding meaning to it through ideals and ideologies. A leaf, an unknown insect, a day—how they live life is truly how life should be lived, without becoming fodder to ideologies, without being torn apart between them. Not by looking to the few great deeds—perhaps I will never accomplish a single act of greatness—but by looking to the myriad and ordinary do we learn of life: *All work is merely work.* They never let you live out just the unadulterated life. We were not born into this life to spend it kowtowing before ideologies.

A Pocketful of Cashews

After accepting on the palm of his hand the bag of cashews he had bought for his son, Rajman once again stepped into the darkness of a blackout. He now walked with the knowledge of a comradeship and warm possessiveness arising from the privilege of grasping and caressing the fifty-gram weight and plastic sleekness of a fistful of cashews. He crossed a drugstore, a cave of brightness created by damming and preventing light from spilling out into the street, and the doors of a rice-and-oil shop shuttered since some time. On the chest of a dark building erect above him were smeared three rectangles of a grimy, pale glow. Along the street ahead was barely a smattering of lights to count. 'I'll walk slowly; let it take longer.' He enjoyed his cleverness. Joy wafted about him like vapour.

'One is meant to walk home slowly—walking as slowly as I do now—keeping nothing on the mind, making it empty and weightless. I would run to the office in the morning, and run home around this time. That routine brings a sharp ache in the knees. I'll walk slowly. Let it take longer.' Really—it was the *let it take longer* that really pleased him. Trying to really pin down the idea, and with an insight, he said—'Let it take longer.' The joy spilled into the darkness, evaporated in filigrees, and dissipated. But it hadn't floated away very far. He walked with caution, to avoid startling the joy, like a man on tiptoes around a new hen.

Many rushing bodies hurtled past; he gave way to none. He marched ahead, planting his feet with conviction, and nobody ran into him. A small man nearly knocked into him, but he caught hold of him and gently set him aside, and that made him feel magnified. He had been feeling inflated for some time now: the being within him found mysterious the processes through which a man suddenly finds himself growing in stature. He made himself even taller against some passers-by.

He swerved at a familiar spot; the road curved there. The stairs climbing down to the road had spilt there instead, he suffered the injustice of having to surrender a path. As he charted the black lines made by rain-washed soil and dug his heels into the asphalt and marched ahead for fifteen steps, he thought of nothing. 'It takes effort to think of nothing.' After that, he didn't think of anything. His calves, exposed under the inadequate overcoat, were cold. He remembered his hands, shoved into pockets on either side. In the right pocket were the plastic bag of his 'self' and a cold handkerchief. He bestowed the handkerchief to the possessionless left pocket: an act of justice performed by the subconscious, a generous deed. 'There is a blackout,' his mind echoed what was already known to it—it must have been enjoying itself.

He massaged hard with the palm of his hand the smooth film of plastic, as if scouring a vessel, slipping and sliding his fingers over it. He was compelled to walk on, standing erect through the darkness. The cashews were his joys for the day, this bagful of cashew nuts. He wished to take it out and look at it.

It was pitch dark.

His happiness arose from the fact that he now possessed cashews—'It seems I am ecstatic!' He saw a lamp with a large bulb wearing a miniskirt of darkness—Freud's sexual satire. That lamp should always be whirling, like a mantra-inscribed mani wheel at a Buddhist temple. 'I really admire Buddha,' he had said. 'Buddha's simplicity is admirable,' he had said to Ranveer, 'Buddha's simple prescriptions are good.'

'Don't others have it?' Ranveer had scolded him. 'It's just that you're incapable of appreciating clever men.'

In the darkness another self within him emerged laughing heartily, and walked another ten paces, still laughing. He had never eaten a bag of cashews by himself. His body slackened on the road—'I never did eat it.' He had already become a youth and then a man while still harbouring the greed to some day buy a loaf of bread and eat it all by himself; even as he goofed about, incredibly, an enormous 'tragedy' had already precipitated. 'A man's youth is spent so quickly.' He had wanted to drink milk worth two rupees. But in the rush to grow up and become a man he had forgotten to do it. So many desires had died, deprived of regular attention. 'If I had done it—I would have had done it today.' His father would come home drunk, wake up his siblings, him—he would hand them puris, laddoos, rasdaana and nimki, spread on a newspaper, and make them eat, even if in half-sleep. One of his younger brothers would cry as he ate. When he had had the opportunity to eat, those nights were the only memory he had of really eating. 'Mother fed us every morning and evening, but we forget that. We forgot that,' he was saying elatedly—he had become a similar father himself. 'Cashew nuts are delicious.' He tasted it on his teeth, at the base of the tongue.

His teeth were coated with the cream of ground cashew; the base of the tongue was plastered with the thick, white cream. The mouth sensed the nuttiness of roasted cashews; its smell unfurled in the mouth: the aroma of the salted white nut, the sappy wood of magnolia, ink, the waft rising up off the earth after a hot sun. He had clamped shut his jaws, trapping the tongue.

He felt the urge to take out one cashew nut and eat it. He didn't know whether he walked slowly or quickly, he just kept striding obliviously.

In the instance when his face bathed in the wanton harsh white lights of an open sweets shop he heard—'Don't bring home all sorts of sweets for the children. They develop a bad habit, they'll stay up waiting, refusing to go to bed.' He had walked quite a distance since acquiring this knowledge. His Kamal waited for him similarly on this day—he opened his mouth in joy—his son Kamal, only recently recuperated after a bout of typhoid, waited for him, awake. 'What do you want to eat? What shall I bring you?' he had asked in the morning.

'I want cashew nuts.' The boy had been dreaming of it for some time.

'Write it down on a piece of paper and put it in my notebook—I won't forget it,' he had instructed, called his son to his side, and made him write with his own pen—'Cashew nuts.' He kicked aside the obstacles put before his eyes by the blackout—My son is waiting!—and continued walking.

A man was reading a cinema poster in the roving light of his torch. Rajman was suddenly gripped by the need to know the time. There was no benefit in knowing the time—'I'll reach home soon.' His son must be looking at the watch, frequently. He was filled with the joy of fulfilment. Now, he slowed down his feet. His heart even smiled a little in the dark. For some reason he was muttering: 'Routine life is full of terror.' He saw his home in the light that filled his eyes.

'When they open the door, I'll go inside. I'll pretend as if I didn't bring anything; I'll take off the overcoat and throw it over the chair. He will have come to stand by my side. I'll suddenly remember and point to the overcoat pocket. I'll tell him look in the overcoat pocket.'

'I took one out and tasted your cashew,' I'll tell my son, 'Cashews are tasty. One day, I'll buy a packet and eat it all.'

Rajman felt the plastic bag. The curled cashews shifted about. He caressed them some more. Turned the packet around, measured it. It was nearly square, crinkled at the sealed mouth.

'What will I achieve by eating one cashew nut? Cashews are tasty, but my age for tasty treats has passed. I should be able to let go. I am a father, I live for my son—I worked so hard to save him.' He remembered the debts for the medicine, for the doctor. He remembered that he hadn't had a suit tailored that year. 'I have become really weak on the inside, but the world doesn't know it,' a fear gripped him. His colleagues who earned the same salary were always at the billiard hall or laughing at their losses at card games, and managed to entertain women. If someone bought him a drink one evening, he would have to buy everybody a round at another time. 'No—I must think only of my family!'

The cold light pooled inside a shop, the dark street that

came flowing forth, the grains of starlight in the sky—he observed everything and kept walking. But he couldn't dare look up at the sky again—no, not at all.

He was still holding the cashews. The greed to eat just one cashew nut was still there, and he was still holding the cashews. Darkness had clotted and thickened there. It was wet, adhesive. His heart was crying, sobbing. His foot stepped on a crack on the street, he searched for more cracks to step on and didn't find one immediately. 'I'll step on them! I will!' Then he became afraid to step just anywhere. Eventually, he froze suddenly and became terrified of walking. 'Duty!' A few figures were approaching from the distance, in the dark. He began mechanically walking again. His lesser self, standing guard against the outer world, had been crying. 'I am still holding the cashews. I'm gripping them even harder now; they will break,' he experienced that fear, and worried that it would be embarrassing. He loosened his grip, as if around a kitten, and examined if it had died, turned it over and around. He felt that the bag was giving up its ghost.

He showed affection to the bag of cashews just as he would his son, and repeatedly caressed it.

The buildings that had come out in the blackout sat up one after the other, with their English shapes and impenetrability, steeped in the blackness of the night. 'The son is waiting—my son—for me, for the cashew nuts. I have never brought home a whole bag of cashews for him before. Today, I have brought a whole bag, just for him.' In satisfaction, he laughed: joy for the dark minutes that had passed. His chest swelled with determination. 'Life must be secured against irregularities.'

In the village below, the dancing light of a fire from

one house entered another house, separated by only a small distance, washing the room in red. The room was bathed in red. He enjoyed the blaze of ringed light. The flames on the fire died down, but he continued watching—he had become a person with two large disks for eyes, a spoonful of brain, a pair of tongs for legs. He continued to walk and stare into the same darkness.

'How do I open this bag, Baba?' he heard his son ask. 'The entire bag is yours,' he would reply.

He became euphoric with himself, he remained overjoyed. A filigree of a sentence spoke in his mind—'I have brought you an entire bag, son.'

'I almost ate one of your cashew nuts, I nearly tore into the bag.' He patted his young son's small knees and said, 'I am not being happy because I managed to bring it to you without ripping it open; that's an old matter, that is something else—something you'll understand when you become a father yourself. But today, I'm putting the entire bag in your hands.'

He had never eaten a whole bag of cashews by himself, Rajman remembered something he had managed to forget, but the memory encountered the exultation careening about in his heart and was obliterated.

He had arrived home. The dog got up, barked, whined and whimpered and lolled up to him. In the electric light on the black curtain raised over the top half of the entrance he recognized the shape of his son's head.

'Knock! Knock! Open the door!' he called out from afar, checked to make sure that all four corners of the packet were intact, adopted the gait of a colossus, and walked into the house.

Power of a Dream

If a dream can be reined and commandeered to a purpose at will, it can transform into power. At such a time, it becomes the third element, obedient to the pair of thought and invention, and thus the most helpful faculty for an individual. Here, a long and cautious study of the subconscious by a psychoanalyst is imperative. But, nature, fatigued sometimes with the monotony of her products, seems sometimes to arbitrarily bestow this gift unto somebody...

One night, Man Bahadur saw in his dream a man he had never laid eyes on, never met.

In Man Bahadur's own words:

I had never before seen the man anywhere, neither had I ever read of a character like him. The man, nearly six feet tall, wearing red shoes, khaki trousers, a jacket with green stripes and a felt hat, was striding in my direction, not looking at me or paying any attention, overtaking all other pedestrians. When he reached quite close, I carefully studied his face. The dream muddied there for an instance. When it became clearer, he was addressing me:

'I owe you ten rupees, don't I? If I say I'll pay you back, I'll make sure to keep my word. If I'd known I'd need the money right now, I would have carried it on me.'

'Well, when will you pay me?' I asked impatiently. He turned his dark, flat face with its slender, pointed nose and a bright pair of eyes and said, 'I shall always carry a ten-rupee note on me. Whenever you meet me next, just ask, and I promise to give it to you. If I go back on my words, may a jeep run me over and kill me.'

The man looked very scared as he took the oath.

In the morning, as I watered the flowers in my garden, I quizzed over what portents the dream might contain. Because it is said that money is a nest of strife, I worried that I might quarrel with someone during the day and so became careful.

I was walking towards my workplace, taking care to keep to the edge of the road, when I reached the exact spot that I had seen in my dream. People walked past. I paused to carefully examine the spot. If I were to get into a quarrel, this would be just the place. But everybody was quietly walking about their own business. I counted myself a fool and continued on my road. Just then, I saw a man was approaching me from the distance. He was wearing a double-breasted green coat and khaki trousers with rounded cuffs. He was surely scared in a big way, and was crossing the road in a hurry. I came to a puzzled halt. He was also wearing a felt hat, but he just wouldn't look in my direction. When he came very close I carefully scanned his face. It was the same man! I wasn't in the least scared; instead, I was overcome by a desire to play mischief. 'I am going to try and ask him for money,' I thought.

I hurried after him, matching strides, until I stopped him and said, 'Give me my ten rupees.'

The man stared at me with wide-open eyes. Then he examined me from head to toe. He comprehended nothing. He tried to ask me something but his parted lips merely trembled a little. Then he took a step backward. I continued to stare him down, as if I'd swallow him whole. One of his hands tentatively went inside the coat, took out a green ten-rupee note, and he quietly handed it to me.

I took the money and walked away.

Right up until the post-office hid me around a bend, I felt as if he had turned around to watch me.

I told nobody about that incident. I was afraid that people would listen to the story and make all sorts of comments, add to it and exaggerate it into a different story. But I would, without fail and every day, take out the ten-rupee note and inspect it. Worried that it was a fake, I even compared the serial number to the list of serial numbers for counterfeit currency written down in my notebook. The note wasn't a fake. A few days later I began to suspect: 'Can I use this to buy something?' On that day, I bought a book with it. The shopkeeper accepted it and put it in his box. I screamed in panic and asked for the note to be returned. I gave another note in exchange and ran homewards.

I spent the night in trepidation, worried that perhaps my secret was fraying at the edges, slowly being revealed to the world.

The man wasn't seen in my dreams again. I didn't run into him during the day either. Occasionally, I would go to the police station to ask if there was news about anybody being run over and killed by a jeep. Later, I felt as if the constables at the station had become suspicious of me. Worried that my secret could become exposed there, and out of caution, I no longer visited the police station.

Just when it seemed everything had become tranquil, he appeared right at my door one early morning. He had become very skinny. He also became very frightened upon seeing me. But I only felt anger. Because I had to face him again.

'Don't be upset to see me,' he came nearer and said in a pitiable voice. 'Are you angry because you have to return the ten rupees? But you do have to return that!'

'No! You won't get a single paisa!'

'Why won't I?' he continued in a polite but firm voice. 'Explain to me why I gave you those ten rupees!'

I was hard pressed for an answer.

'You tell me—why did you give it to me? You must have had a reason to, otherwise why would you? Explain to me the accounts between us, and if I owe you that money, I will give it to you right now. If I go back on my word, may a truck run me over and kill me!'

He stood there, with the light gone out of his face.

I left for the bazaar.

He returned the next day, just as early in the morning. He pottered around in the yard for nearly half an hour, waiting.

'It's only because I don't have anything at home to eat! How can you toy with a man's life!' He was on the verge of tears. 'Give me the money. Right now. I'll buy rice.'

I really was beginning to toy with him. I repeated my old lines.

'Show me the accounts first. Show me what I owe you—I'll definitely give you the money then. But don't be a child and whine that someone else's money is yours. It just can't be true that I have borrowed a measly ten rupees from you.'

As he was leaving, he said—'Enjoy it! I hope you get fat on the ten rupees you have tricked out of me. You're toying with me now, but you'll come to regret my murder someday. Some hooligan you are! I may die, but I'll show you...'

A few days after that I met him on the same road. He didn't speak to me. He scuttled away along the edge of the road. I had kept his money in my pocket. I had grown attached to the money. The day when I would have to part with it, I would...

A week later, as I was walking to work, I saw him approaching with a friend. His friend was distinguished by his fur hat and police boots. Even though I pretended not to notice, I saw him pucker his mouth to point me out to the friend. The things he must be saying to slander me! I tried hard to ignore them. The fur hat sniggered as he passed. But I didn't lose my patience. I walked along my road, not paying them any heed.

From the next day on, I didn't dream of the man or run into him in person. Nine or ten months passed, and he still didn't appear. A certain regret started nagging me. What if he really had had nothing to eat? Did I bring about his ruin? If only I could meet him, I would... I desperately searched for him, but I never found him. And then something new happened: I even forgot his face, how it looked. Then I became absolutely convinced that he had already died.

I inquired about him with many people—perhaps someone knew where he used to work. I went to the hospital, but nobody had been run over by a jeep.

Something had started gnawing at me from the inside. I was always afraid that I would descend into psychosis, that

I would lose my mind later. A lifelong attachment to this ten-rupee note would remain, surely; but if I were unable to return it, I would possibly become increasingly deranged with each passing day. I desperately needed to talk to somebody about my condition. If only I could reach his grave and howl to my heart's content...

I suddenly remembered the fur-hat. I must find him, I thought—to meet him was to resolve all issues...

In the morning, I stood at the same spot along the road. Fur-hat didn't pass that way.

He didn't show up the next day either.

I was waiting on the third day. And, surely, he approached from the distance. As he walked, he halted, hesitated, as if to make sure that I saw him.

'Where is your friend?' I rushed to his side and asked breathlessly.

He hesitated.

'Where is your friend? Where is he?' I asked anxiously. And, in the excitement, I had his arm in a tight grip, as if I was worried that he would run away and disappear forever.

'Which friend?' he asked instead.

'Your friend! He walked with you through here one day.'

'Who could it be?'

'Quit dithering! The one in the khaki trousers, a green coat, and a felt hat...'

'He wasn't a friend of mine.'

'Whoever he is—where is he now?'

'He died.'

'He died?'

'Been two months now.'

I let go of his arm.

'He had no job, no money—he starved to death. He fell ill, but he must have thought it better to put a clean end to it rather than waste away in bed. He killed himself by jumping off the cliff at Kagebhir,' he said.

I couldn't muster anything more to say.

When I went to bed that night the sights of Kagebhir kept flooding into my eyes. What would people think of me if I go there in the day and scream? But I reached Kagebhir in my dream.

It was moonlit.

The tall, naked and dark trunk of an Indian trumpet tree. He clutched bags full of banknotes and stood at the precipice.

I looked down the cliff. It was a rocky outcrop, scraggly with clumps of bracken. There I shouted, 'I never got to know who you were. I have your ten rupees. Dreams enchanted me. That is the only reason why I didn't return your money. You shouldn't have had to die. I really have grown attached to your banknote. But if anybody asks for it I will return your money to him.'

I was still thinking of what else I could say to him when a man emerged from the base of an alder.

'How could I be dead? I only pretended to die, just to get the money. Fur-hat taught me everything and sent me to you,' he laughed. 'So, will you return my money now?'

I was also laughing.

When the laughter ceased I took out his banknote from my pocket, offered it to him, and said, 'Oh, take it right away! God! Your money! There's no way I am going to hold on to it anymore.'

When he saw the banknote in my hand he jumped as far away as he could, as if he had discerned the outlines of a treacherous plot.

'I won't take this banknote. This note I won't take, not now, no way!'

I threw the note to the ground and said, 'Once it has left my pocket, it can't return. The money is there. Pick it, keep it. I'm leaving! See!'

The man screamed. 'I absolutely refuse to take this money today. If you force me, I'll really jump off this cliff and kill myself.'

And, what if, when he jumps off the cliff in this dream, what if he dies in real life, in the bed where he is sleeping right now? A new anxiety smothered me.

'All right then. I will keep it for the night, but take it away tomorrow,' I said, and picked up the banknote.

Early this morning somebody knocked on the door.

It was the same man.

'Return the ten rupees,' he proudly demanded.

I was astonished. But I said in a steady voice, 'Why did you refuse to take the money when I offered it to you last night?'

'Aren't you a clever one!' he said bravely. 'You'd borrow my money in reality and try to return it in dreams!'

I felt as if I had vaguely understood something. My head hurt. I squeezed out a final question, 'Do you want the same banknote, or can I give you another note?'

He replied with ease, 'Give me whatever you want. But don't give me bad money.'

Acknowledgements

I am immensely grateful to Mr Indra Bahadur Rai for trusting me with the task of translating these stories. I have but succeeded in capturing a fraction of the grace, density and economy of his original. I also acknowledge the hard work and courage of translators who have translated some of these stories before, and I invite other translators to create new translations of I. B. Rai's short stories, in English and in other languages.

Anurag Basnet—I wouldn't have been able to muster the courage to attempt translating these stories without you in my corner. My friends and fellow editors at *La.Lit*, along with Nepali writers and poets who have allowed me to translate their works, are always a source of inspiration.

A new generation of readers in Nepal and abroad will have access to a small share of I. B. Rai's works. My hope is that this book will encourage new readers to explore more of Mr Rai's literary legacy, and also push more readers towards becoming translators and emissaries between languages and cultures.